THE
WHITE ROOM

Zoran Živković

The White Room
Copyright © 2022 by Zoran Živković

ISBN: 978-4-908793-54-7

Cover: Youchan Ito, Togoru Art Works

Neoclassic Fleurons font used with permission of
Paulo W–Intellecta Design

Cadmus Press
cadmusmedia.org

THE
WHITE ROOM

Zoran Živković

Translated from the Serbian
by
Randall A. Major

Cadmus Press
2022

To Alyosha, my grandson

IVANA HAD GONE MISSING.

I discerned this gradually, as the evening wore on.

As usual, I finished teaching my creative writing class at nine. After the eight attendees who gather at my place at seven o'clock on a Tuesday had left, I put my study in order and went into the kitchen to prepare supper for Ivana and myself. The evening meal was our only chance to eat together on workdays. It rarely occurred that we were not together at the dining table at the same time in the evening. Though she was not currently at home, I expected her soon. She knows that I am fairly hungry after class, because on those days when I have no students, we generally eat at around half past seven.

I did not know where she had gone. Ivana always tells me where she is going—as I also tell her—but today she had not done so because there were special circumstances. I was in quite a bind timewise, so as she left she had not wanted to bother me with what she might be able to tell me upon returning.

IT SEEMED THAT CIRCUMSTANCES had been conspiring against me since that morning. It should have been a quiet day, but unexpected duties and unannounced visits kept devouring my time. Thus, instead of my usual practice of preparing classes in the morning, I only got to it at the last moment: it was already ten minutes after five when I finally settled down to work on a task which would usually take at least an hour and a half to complete.

Fifteen minutes later, I was roused from my contemplations by a wispy kiss on the top of my head, almost without a touch. I was slightly startled because I had not heard Ivana at all as she approached me from behind. I turned around and saw that she was dressed to go out.

I gave her a quizzical look, but she only flashed me a lipstick-laden smile, waved wordlessly, and left.

It took me about ten minutes to warm up the ready-made food in the microwave, prepare a salad, and set the dining room table. Ivana, however, was still not here. What is keeping her, I wondered as I went to my study for my cell phone. Only then did it occur to me that she had perhaps texted or called me if something out of the ordinary had happened, and that I had not heard because I turn my ringtone off during class.

The little green lamp on the upper right-hand corner of the phone was not blinking, which meant there had been no calls, messages, or e-mails. I turned the ringtone back on, then called Ivana. A female voice answered, but not hers: "The number you have dialed is not available. Please try again later."

That was odd. Ivana is extremely careful that her phone does not ring in the wrong place—at the movies, for example, the theater, a concert, a lecture, or wherever she does not want to be disturbed. However, she would just turn off the ringtone, not the telephone itself. Quiet vibrations would inform her of incoming calls and messages. What had led her to stray from her routine?

I had no way of establishing that, so I just had to wait patiently until she returned. Soon, I hoped. My stomach was now grumbling. I went back to the dining room, sat before my empty plate, and stared longingly at the delicious food in front me as it inevitably grew tepid. I restrained myself stoically for about ten minutes, then started eating before it went completely cold.

I soothed my conscience by thinking that Ivana would not mind if I started without her. Should I have to suffer hunger just because something had prevented her from arriving on time? And there must be a simple explanation as well for the phone being off. Her battery might have died, for example. That, to be honest, had never happened to her but, as they say, there is a first time for everything. It is remarkable, I thought with my mouth full, how a person experiencing discomfort such as, let us say, hunger, easily finds an excuse to get their needs met…

Having satiated my initial craving, I continued eating at a slower pace. Even more slowly than usual. By lingering, I wanted to give Ivana another chance to get back, perhaps, before I finished, so that we could at least dine together briefly. As I brought my meal to an end thus, as if forcing myself to eat something that I really was not enjoying, my ever-fuller stomach was driving out the hunger pangs, and the weak spots began to appear in my excuses.

Truth be told, her battery could have died, but hers was not the only telephone in town. Why had she not called me from another phone? She didn't know my cell number by heart? Possibly. We remember ever fewer things nowadays as we depend more on our cell phones, so when they fail, we remain helpless. Nevertheless, she could have called me on the landline. Even if she didn't know that number either, she could find out through the information service.

I stared for a time at the empty plate in front of me, and finally made peace with fate: there would be no meal together. I returned the cooled dish of food into the refrigerator, together with the salad, but I left Ivana's plate, glass, and silverware on the table. When she did finally arrive home, she would surely be hungry and just warm her supper up again in the microwave. That is, of course, if she had not eaten somewhere else already...

I washed the dishes I had used and, not knowing what better to do, sat down in my armchair and took a book that I had begun reading a few days before—Laurent Binet's excellent novel *The Seventh Function of Language*. I was captivated by the enthralling story and became engrossed in my reading. After fifty-odd pages, I looked at the digital clock on the shelf; it was a quarter to eleven. Indeed, good fiction can deceive one's sense of time: I had read for more than an hour, but I had the impression that only twenty minutes had passed.

And not only that. My guilty conscience also jabbed me when I realized that the whole time I was residing enthralled in the parallel world of this novel, I had not given Ivana a single thought. That was certainly a compliment to Binet, but an unforgivable transgression towards Ivana, to whom something had certainly happened. Not one single explanation crossed my mind for the fact that it was, my goodness, nearly eleven, and she was not home and had not called. As if the earth had swallowed her whole. As if she had simply disappeared.

A wave of panic rushed through me. A whole series of useless thoughts crossed my mind: I should go search for her (*yes, but where?*), I should report her disappearance on social media (*yes, but I do not use any, I do not know how that is done*), I should call her brother or aunt (*yes, but I do not even have their phone numbers*), I should ask our mutual friends if anyone had heard anything about her (*I would just unnecessarily disturb them at this late hour; if anyone had heard something, they surely would have called by now*), I should contact the hospitals (*yes, but they do not give out information unless you are related to the patient or*—I became petrified—*the deceased*)...

Once I had recovered myself a little, the very thing I should have first thought of as a fan and occasional writer of detective fiction then dawned on me: when someone goes missing, you do nothing under your own initiative, but instead report the case to the police. The sooner, the better.

2

"ONE MOMENT PLEASE, I'LL connect you with the inspector on duty," the rather young female voice answered me from the switchboard, after I had briefly stated why I was calling and answered her question as to where I was calling from.

This time, the voice was a bit older, but still female. "Senior Inspector Sanja Mrvaljević."

"Good evening. Zoran Živković here…" I paused, and in my confusion, unnecessarily added, "Professor… I wish to…"

"And writer?" she interrupted me inquiringly.

"That, too," I responded with a touch of hesitation, as if mention of it made me uncomfortable.

"How can I help you, Professor Živković?"

"I would like to report… a missing person."

"What's their name?"

"Ivana… Ivana Đurić."

The muffled sound of typing on a keyboard could be heard. "Are you somehow related to Ivana Đurić?"

"Yes… in fact, no… well, it's as if I were… though not formally… We have been together… for a while now… almost two years."

"I understand. Do you know her date of birth, please?"

"Of course. July 10, 1969."

Typing again.

"She resides in Šajkaška Street?"

"She is registered but does not live there. She sublet her apartment. We have been living at my place for about a year. My address is…"

"I can see where you live," Inspector Mrvaljević interrupted me, typing all the while. "We're neighbors."

"You also live in this neighborhood?"

"I work here. At the Novi Beograd police station. Could you please give me Ms. Đurić's telephone number?"

"Just a moment." I checked my telephone's address book and dictated the number to her. "It is of no use to you," I added. "Her cell phone is off."

"Even if it's off, it can be useful. What makes you think that Ms. Đurić is missing?"

"She was supposed to return two hours ago. If she were detained somewhere, she would have called me by now. And she never turns off her cell phone. Something has most certainly happened to her."

"When did you last see her?"

I reflected for a moment. "Around five-thirty, just before she left."

"Where was she headed?"

"I don't know. She didn't tell me."

"Is that normal—that she doesn't say where she's going?"

"No, far from it. Today was different. She didn't wish to disturb me while I was working. Every minute counted. I was late. I was preparing for my class at seven. Creative writing…"

"One of my friends went to your classes."

"It really is a small world. What is her name?"

"How was Ms. Đurić dressed?" the senior inspector responded with a question.

I had to think again. "Like always…"

"I remember my friend telling me that you would reprimand them if they gave such a vague description of a character. It's the same in my job. 'Like always' doesn't mean anything to me…"

I sighed. "She was wearing an overcoat…"

"She would hardly go out in the middle of winter without an overcoat. What color was it? What kind of shoes was she wearing? Did she have on a cap, or a scarf maybe? Was she carrying a purse? An umbrella? Was she dressed up?"

I shook my head remorsefully. "I don't remember. I was completely focussed on correcting the stories. I only gave Ivana a glance…"

"Your Inspector Lukić has a much better eye for details." From the sound of her voice, I would say she was smiling.

"I am flattered that you know about Inspector Lukić, but I certainly was not the model for that character. To the contrary. That would much more likely have been Ivana. If the situation were reversed, if I had gone missing and she were talking with you now, you would receive the most detailed description possible."

"Then, maybe in a new novel you could have a lady-inspector as your heroine."

"New novels are not a problem. Let us first find Ivana."

"We'll do our best. I'll call as soon as I have news for you. Soon, I hope. You're not going to bed imminently?"

"How could I?"

3

As I CLEARED THE dining table, I was weighed down
by the feeling that I was turning my back on Ivana.
As if I were demonstrating that I no longer counted
on her to return home that evening. My rather quaint
predilection for orderliness, however, outweighed my
conscience. I took comfort in the idea that I could easily return the dishes to the table if she showed up and
felt hungry.

I settled back into the armchair and re-opened *The
Seventh Function of Language*, but I didn't get far. I
would read five or six lines of the lengthy and complicated introductory paragraph to the new chapter, but
then be forced to return to the beginning because absolutely nothing of it remained in my mind. After several
such fruitless attempts, I finally surrendered.

I continued sitting in the armchair with the book in
my lap, waiting for Senior Inspector Mrvaljević to call
me. I had no notion how long it might take before she
had news for me. She had said that she hoped it would
be soon, but that was a relatively indefinite adverb of
time.

I had written a trilogy about Inspector Lukić, but in
fact knew very little about the actual workings of the
police. A protocol for missing-person cases certainly
exists. Most likely, they check first if the missing person has been admitted to any of the hospitals. If they

are not located there—what then? I strained to figure out what they might undertake next, but my writing and other forms of ingenuity have never been up to par at such a late hour, not to mention the mental state in which I found myself.

Thus, overwhelmed above all by my frustration at being helpless to do anything for Ivana, I surrendered to my only remaining, and least satisfying, option: an indefinite waiting period. While I was reading, time had passed quickly, but now it reverted to the other extreme—it seemed to creep by. The red numerals on the digital clock changed with intolerable slowness.

As midnight edged closer, fatigue began to overcome me. Had the situation not been extraordinary, I would already have been between the sheets. Even though I attempted gallantly to remain awake, staring at the clock slowly put me to sleep. When the phone did finally ring, I was roused from the slumber into which I had imperceptibly slipped. A quick glance at the clock told me that I had slept only a few minutes, but I felt ashamed nevertheless. Before answering, I quickly cleared my throat so I would not sound groggy.

"It took a while, Professor Živković, but I have good news," Senior Inspector Mrvaljević said.

"You found Ivana?" I almost exclaimed, suddenly wide awake.

"No, but it's almost certain that she's all right."

"Almost certain?"

"Yes. First of all, we checked central reporting—not a single reported event after five-thirty mentions the name of Ms. Đurić. Then we called emergency services and the on-duty hospitals. There's nothing about her there either."

"What if," I interrupted her, "they could not... identify her? She could have lost her papers… she might have been mugged, for example."

"There have been no anonymous patients this evening. In the end, we also checked with customs and immigration—she didn't leave the country."

"You didn't have to do that," I said self-confidently. "Where would Ivana go abroad so suddenly? Besides, how could she go without her passport?"

"She could easily have taken it if she intended to travel. You surely wouldn't have noticed, busy or not busy."

"But where would she go and what would she do in a foreign country?"

"I don't know, but I do know that almost a fifth of those reported as missing persons turn up somewhere abroad. Anyway, that's not the case here. Ms. Đurić is still in Serbia."

"Good, but that does not mean she is all right. Something might have happened to her, only the police don't know about it and she just hasn't managed to reach the hospital. For example, what if she has been kidnapped? That is not a rare occurrence, is it?"

"It isn't very frequent either. And what do you suppose could be the reason for her kidnapping? She is too far along in years to be of interest to those who deal in sex trafficking."

"Hold on there, Ivana is quite a beautiful and attractive woman…"

"She surely is, but in that business even thirty-year-olds are considered too old."

"Maybe they kidnapped her for blackmail," I persisted.

"If that were so, the blackmailers would already have called. Besides, Professor Živković, the rich are kidnapped. Don't get me wrong, but those would be some really naïve kidnappers if they hoped to get any sort of ransom from a Serbian writer. Anyhow, none of that's important. Ms. Đurić definitely hasn't been kidnapped. She went to the place where she is of her own free will."

"Where is that?"

"That, unfortunately, I'm not allowed to say."

"Why are you not allowed?" I asked in bewilderment. "I don't understand…"

"Because I don't have the right to. If Ms. Đurić were a minor, and you her father or guardian, then I could tell you where she is. As it is, she is certainly of age, she's free to go wherever she wants. There has been no violation of the law, and the police are not private detectives. It's important you know that nothing bad has happened to her, and she will contact you if and when she decides to. I'm sorry I can't help you any more than that. I hope you understand me."

For several long moments I did not know how to respond.

"Could you at least tell me," I finally said, "how you found her?"

Now it was Senior Inspector Mrvaljević's turn to fall briefly silent.

"Using recordings from closed-circuit cameras." It was as if her voice was slightly muffled. "Starting from those covering the surroundings of the building where you live. She went out around five-thirty, just as you told me. It wasn't hard to follow her. Since recent times, the city's been well-covered by cameras. Ultimately she arrived at her intended destination. Nothing unfortunate happened to her on the way." She paused slightly, then went on. "She's still there. That's all I can tell you."

"That is horrible!" I let fly, out of sheer perplexity and

anger. "That is total police surveillance." I immediately regretted it, but it was too late. It really was not the inspector's fault that she couldn't reveal more to me. She had otherwise been most obliging. And she had read at least one of my books...

I was just about to apologize, but she forestalled me.

"There's no reason to complain. If it wasn't for that 'total police surveillance', as you call it, we wouldn't know the whereabouts of Ms. Đurić. And life has taught me that it's always better to know even those things that are unpleasant, rather than be left in the dark." Again she paused briefly. "By the way, she's wearing a long grey overcoat, with a sash. She has a thick dark red woolen scarf, a beret of the same color, black ankle boots, and she's carrying a rather large taupe grey purse and a black umbrella. Maybe that will help you. Good night, Professor Živković."

4

I PUT THE BOOK and my cell phone on the desk, stood up, and turned off all the other lights in the apartment except for the one over the armchair. I went back and sat with my legs folded beneath me. I did not go to lie down because I was so wide awake and excited that I would have been unable to fall asleep, and would just have been tossing and turning in bed. And it would be better if Ivana, if she did indeed return, found me here waiting for her than in bed asleep. However, I was not very hopeful that she would come back. Midnight had passed, and her telephone was still turned off.

If only Senior Inspector Mrvaljević had at least revealed Ivana's location to me. Perhaps she would have given me a hint, had I not insulted her with my comment about total police surveillance. I could hear from her voice that I had struck a nerve. And rightly so. If it were not for all those cameras, I would still be afraid that something bad had happened to Ivana. Now I knew that it had not, but that did not quell my fears. Not regarding Ivana's safety, but our relationship.

The first time it crossed my mind that Ivana had perhaps left me was while I hesitated to start eating. Hunger raised a variety of dark thoughts. I easily drove them out as soon as I started to eat. The idea that she had left me, however, now returned and took root. Even more so because I could not think of any other explanation for Ivana's disappearance, since the possibility that she was in trouble had fallen away.

And the senior inspector's words contributed to it—the hint that it is always better to know, even if it is unpleasant, than to be in the dark. Had she seen something in the recordings which drove her to inform me in a roundabout way that a breakup with Ivana was on the horizon? I could only guess at what that might be, but whatever she had seen, the causes which lay behind it were not out there somewhere, but right here. If Ivana had indeed left me, she must have been driven to it by something she could no longer stand in our almost two-year-long relationship.

In the dead silence of night, sitting in my armchair as if in a little boat on a restless sea of uncertainty, I set off in search of the roots of Ivana's dissatisfaction. A profound search, because nothing prominent or obvious came to mind.

5

I had met Ivana about two and a half years ago. A friend of hers, who had been attending my creative writing classes for a while, had convinced Ivana to accompany her. For the first month or two she was noticeably reticent, as if she were rethinking her decision to attend. She would choose to sit in a corner, and almost never spoke up, which was unusual. New attendees are generally more talkative than those who have worked with me longer.

Ivana's very first story revealed that she was remarkably talented. Writing is like singing. I do not have to perform an entire aria for you to conclude that I will never become a singer. It is sufficient for me just to start singing, so you only hear my voice for a few moments. In the same way, I do not have to read your entire novel in order to determine whether your métier is prose or not. For an experienced mentor of creative writing, a short story is quite enough to establish whether its author has or does not have a voice for prose.

Ivana remained peculiarly indifferent to the praises I offered for her first stories. This was also atypical. Knowing that I am not lavish with my compliments, attendees—both callow and seasoned—do not hesitate to show their enthusiasm whenever they receive one. It was only after the third or fourth story, when I asked her outright whether she perhaps felt uncomfortable with my praises, that she finally smiled and shook her head.

To be honest, her stories were not completely on point. Although excellently written, they only loosely kept to the topics I had assigned. Sometimes the deviations were bigger, sometimes smaller, but I did not cavil about it. The themes, in fact, were not really that important. And anyway, I only assign them at the start of the course as a support for new attendees, for whom the biggest headache is inventing topics. And this is true of the majority of students. They wish to write, but they do not know about what. Ivana did know, and she also knew how to write. In any case, all of them eventually become independent in their choice of topic, and the sooner that occurs, the better.

She stopped attending the course as soon as we became closer. (I saw no reason for it, but she had made her decision.) Months later, I asked once, randomly and out of pure curiosity, why she did not stick to the themes I had assigned. I was convinced that she would also write great stories based on them. She answered me after a certain amount of hesitation. Her voice, which had till then been fairly bright and chirpy, suddenly softened and became serious.

The stories were not written on topic because she had stopped writing. Altogether. The stories she sent me had been written earlier, and she had just adapted them slightly to create the illusion that she was more or less keeping to the subject. Confused by her answer and change of tone, I first asked her a less important question: if she had stopped writing, why had she enrolled in a creative writing class?

Again she answered me seriously, and again she surprised me. She wanted to get to know the writer of *The*

Papyrus Trilogy more intimately. Why that particular book? She looked at me silently for a few moments, then shrugged. We had been together long enough by then for me to know that it would be useless to insist. If she ever did decide to answer, she would do so when she thought the time was right. I was answered by another shrug two days later, when I finally remembered to ask her a more important question: why had she stopped writing?

Our relationship had started through a certain freedom of interpretation, and not through any intent or calculation on her part or mine. I liked Ivana, that was certainly true—not just at first sight, but also on a second and deeper look—yet that still wouldn't have been enough for me to take action. Throughout more than a decade of mentoring in creative writing, I had made absolutely sure that my private and professional lives did not intersect. That was not always easy: there had been occasions and challenges—ladies of varying disposition make up the majority of those whom I instruct in the writing of literary prose—but I had been married almost the whole time, and since I am monogamous by nature, I resisted all temptation. Besides, because of my age, I grew less and less attractive in that sense...

Ivana started attending the course in the autumn, and at year's end she announced that she would not be coming to class in the first half of February. She was preparing to travel to Sri Lanka with a friend. For the third year in a row. I told her I envied her for that. For ages I had also wanted to visit Sri Lanka—Arthur Clarke lived there, the writer whose body of work I had focused on in my master's thesis and with whom I had corresponded for years—but a variety of circumstances had prevented me from doing so. It turned out that Ivana was to spend her winter/summer vacation in precisely the little place where Clarke had lived for a long time.

In Ivana's e-mail from Unawatuna, there was a photograph of his house surrounded by palm trees on the shore of the Indian Ocean. Fascinated, using carefully chosen words, I suggested I join her the following year on her next pilgrimage to Sri Lanka, if that were to take place and if I were a desirable traveling companion for her. Was I too selective with my words? Did they hint at something more than an innocent suggestion that we travel together? I do not have the right to decide about that. A writer is the only one who must not interpret what he or she writes, even in a seemingly harmless exchange of correspondence. Nor must they confirm or contest someone else's interpretation.

Upon Ivana's return, we met outside of class for the first time. After the more than two hundred photographs she had shown me, I had the impression that I had been there myself. We continued seeing each other, and almost every parting was comical: we shook hands like business partners. Two or three times, out of doors, I did not even take off my gloves because it was so cold. Finally, on March 20, we stopped shaking hands.

I did not, however, therefore stop being monogamous, even though I was still married then. For months, I had not been living with my second wife, a Frenchwoman, and the divorce was being finalized.

Although we were in the throes of romantic elation that accompany the start of a relationship, Ivana and I had to answer some practical and principal questions. One of the first somehow answered itself. We decided to go on living in our own apartments. We mostly saw each other at my place, but Ivana most often slept at her place on workdays. It was easier for her to run from there to work at the governmental office in Slavija. We spent the weekends in Novi Beograd, and it just so happened that I never slept at her place in Dorćol.

It seems there will never be a chance for me to do so, because after about a year Ivana decided to simplify her life by moving in with me and renting out her apartment. From Novi Beograd she could no longer walk to work or back when public transport was overcrowded, but in every other sense life together was more practical. And living under the same roof confronted us with a primary issue that we had not faced before. Not because either of us avoided it, but simply because it had not come up yet.

As her fiftieth birthday approached, she told me, just by the way, in the middle of some other conversation, that she only had a little more time left to get married. Ivana, it should be said, had had two long-term relationships, but neither of them was conjugal. I gave her a confused look. A little more time? Yes, it makes sense to get married before you're fifty. After that, not so much. Why would it not make sense to get married after fifty? People get married even in their nineties. She shrugged, which, if I understood correctly, this time meant that there was no reason to explain to me something which was self-explanatory. Whose fault was it that something so obvious was not clear to me?

She never broached the topic again, but I did. I had the need to justify myself, even though she was blaming me for nothing. Firstly, I deprecated myself. The fact that I was twice-divorced certainly did not recommend me for a new marriage. I could claim as loudly as I wanted that I was not at fault for my divorces, but it was certain that my two former wives were also convinced of their innocence. Then I tried to make light of it by citing someone who said that a second marriage is the triumph of hope over experience, and the third the triumph of madness over hope and experience. Since Ivana did not find this funny, I grew serious and asked her what would change if we were married. What was wrong with the way things were?

She looked me straight in the eye for some time before she answered, "Nothing."

It was my turn to look her in the eye for some time, then I opened my heart. The significant difference in our ages was a major argument against marriage. If I were fifty and she thirty, that would all be fine. But I had already embarked upon my seventy-third year. Before Ivana lay two very high-quality decades—precisely that time of life when I, alongside other things, had written most of my books. And what lay before me? If I was lucky, another six or seven years of healthy living, then, inevitably, old age and all that goes with it. And in no way did I want anyone—Ivana least of all—to be saddled with my old age. Which is what would happen if we were married.

She broke out crying over this. Ivana is prone to tears anyway, she starts crying when we watch a romantic comedy, so I did not get overly upset. It would pass. In any case, I had not told her anything bad. She herself confirmed that we were living as if married and, of course, we would stay together. She would not notice that she was not married.

Soon, she wiped away her tears, and then murmured something. I did not quite hear her, so she repeated more clearly, "You really don't understand women."

Now, this did upset me. I do not understand women? If there is anything I am proud of in my prose, it is my female characters. "You would not think that if you had read any of my other books besides *The Papyrus Trilogy.*"

I expected another round of tears, but it did not come. What came was another long look in the eyes, then an announcement made in a solemn promissory tone. "I'll read them. All of them."

6

SINCE THEN, SIX MONTHS had passed and I still had not seen a single one of my books in her hands. Yesterday, I made a passing allusion to it. In the middle of some unimportant conversation, I uttered the unfinished sentence, "When my books finally reach the head of the line…" Her eyes welled up, but she did not start crying.

It would be best if I didn't mention this anymore, I concluded. There is obviously some problem here that is beyond my comprehension. Anyway, this was nothing new. My two former spouses had also had an aversion, for different reasons, to reading my books. Even though I in no way insisted that they be fans of my prose, they experienced as pressure even my silent expectation that they at least read my books, so they, under varying pretenses, offered resistance. It discomfited me, of course, but I made peace with my destiny: I would never be a prophet in my own home. In any case, this circumstance did not contribute at all to either of my divorces.

After yesterday's insignificant unpleasantness, Ivana fell silent and withdrew into herself. Engrossed in one of my tasks, I did not notice it immediately. It took a while to get her into a better mood. It seemed that we had smoothed things over. Neither yesterday nor today was there any more mention of my books.

Now, however, as I sat huddled in the armchair, struggling to comprehend why Ivana would leave me, I wondered if everything truly was all right. What if she was only pretending that it was so, while actually she had reached a point where she could no longer stand living with a writer? I do not experience myself as the incarnation of vanity and conceit, but who knows how I seem in her eyes. On the other hand, what kind of conceit is it to remind her half a year later of her promise that she would read my books? And is that something so unpleasant and difficult that she would rather end the relationship, which was otherwise good in all other respects? No, my books were not at fault here. Something else was afoot.

And then it finally hit me. At Ivana's age, one ends a good relationship only if a better one is on the horizon.

Again the words of Senior Inspector Mrvaljević from the end of our second conversation came back to me. Her allusions and hints suddenly crystallized. For example, when she said that *"she is certainly of age, she's free to go wherever she wants"*—she actually meant *with whomever she wants*. Or the reminder that *"the police are not private detectives"*—meant, in fact, *do not spy on unfaithful spouses or partners*. Only one explanation was possible: the inspector had seen Ivana in the footage meeting with someone, and the way the encounter played out drove away any ambiguity about the nature of their relationship.

Of the two questions which are first asked in such unpleasant situations—"With whom?" and "Why?"—the first did not interest me much. At least not yet. Again the inspector's words helped me guess the answer to the second. Her reproachful account of what Ivana was wearing and carrying. All those things that

I had missed, that I had not noticed, even though she was standing right in front of me. I had committed one of the heaviest violations towards the woman with whom I was in a relationship—I had ceased noticing her, I was taking her for granted. I had been completely unaware of it, but did that exculpate me?

An additional aggravating factor also existed. My inattention was certainly not recent. Last night was not the first time I had failed to notice how Ivana was dressed, what shoes she was wearing or what her hair looked like, leading her to decide on the spot to punish me harshly. It had surely been going on for a while, for months. One does not find a lover overnight.

For myself, I could still find at least an explanation, if not even a justification. I am usually most observant, but only partially. I notice some things perfectly; to others I am almost blind, even if they are not insignificant. Women's hair, for example, or their clothes. This seems improbable especially to ladies, because all of them, without exception, notice those qualities first and best. I explained to Ivana long ago how my observation works; she did not say anything on that occasion, but the disbelief could be seen on her face.

New questions began to arise. I put aside for later some which did not need an immediate answer—such as, for example, did Ivana's somewhat tardy insight that the difference in our ages would, after all, be a larger hurdle for us stand behind it all, so that this issue with my selective perception was just a convenient excuse to solve the problem before it got out of hand. Before I became dependent on her because of my age, when it would be harder for her to leave me.

Practical questions came to the forefront—amongst them, first of all, how to move forward. All right, Ivana had left me, she was now with someone else, nothing else was to be done, but her things were still at my place. She would have to come for them, she needed them. There was not a lot: mostly her clothing, a few books, two pictures, her laptop, several knickknacks, three or four potted plants, and a multitude of large and small things in the bathroom, from which she had almost exiled me.

Then it occurred to me that, as she left last night, she had probably taken some things with her in her suitcase. She had no reason to be concerned that, engrossed in my work, I might notice it. As far as that goes, she could even have moved out. That too would have gone unnoticed.

This was easy to verify. I got out of the armchair rather stiffly because I had sat so long and went first into the bedroom. I pushed aside the sliding door on her side of the closet. Of the multitude of hangers, not one was empty, and the big drawer with various T-shirts and underwear was completely full. In the space for shoes on the floor, there were also no empty spots.

Then I went into the bathroom. As always, I was overwhelmed by the mélange of Ivana's scents: perfumes, creams, oils, soaps... At first glance, nothing was missing from there either. My impression, of course, was unreliable, but one thing was certain: Ivana's toothbrush was in the rose-colored glass above the sink. She could have left everything else, but not that. She took it with her even when we went out for dinner. She could, in fact, have bought a new one along the way, but why would she do that?

Quickly I went to all the other places in the apartment where Ivana's things were. Everything was *in situ*. I stood for a while in a dilemma in the middle of the living room, scratching the top of my head. This could mean that Ivana had decided to start a new life without a single memento of her previous one, without anything that might burden her conscience. But it could also mean that she was not planning any sort of new life, that there simply was no lover to whom she had gone, that something else was brewing.

There was only one way for me to discover what was going on. I went back to my study and picked up my cell phone decisively from the desk. The telephone had memorized the number from which Senior Inspector Mrvaljević had called me. Before I pressed the key to call her back, I checked the clock in the upper right-hand corner: seven minutes to two. It mattered not that it was so late, nor that she had no right to tell me what she had seen. I had to try at least to get something from her, otherwise I would not get a wink of sleep.

First of all, I will apologize once more—I thought as it started to ring—for that thing about police surveillance. Then I will play out the role of a desperate man willing to do anything if he does not find out what is going on. She does not have to say where Ivana is; it will be enough if she just hints at whether she was seen with someone. It would hardly be breaking the law to do so…

The ringing went on, but the senior inspector did not answer. Finally, after the seventeenth ring—there, that is what my observation is good for—the line went dead. I kept the mute cell phone to my ear a while longer, then, thwarted, returned it to the desk. I considered trying to reach her via the police switchboard, as on the first occasion, but that would probably be a waste of time. She would not answer me there either. Evidently, for her, this "case" was closed.

Not knowing what else to do, I sat down once again in the armchair. If I was going to spend a sleepless night, it would be better to do so here than in bed. However, I was wrong. It was barely a few minutes that I sat staring blankly before me, wrapped in the profound peace of night, before I effortlessly slipped off to sleep.

I SQUINTED IN WONDER at my surroundings, as if they were an unreal scene from a dream, and not just an everyday thing. I was in my study, curled up in my armchair. Even though I felt all stiff, I did not rise immediately; I first tried to wake myself up. Obviously, I had fallen asleep there the night before, and morning had long since broken. The window was filled with the bright blue hue of the winter morning sky. The natural light mixed unpleasantly with the artificial one from the lamp which had burned all night above my head. I reached out my tingling hand and turned the light off. I should have gone to bed after all; I had tortured myself unnecessarily in the armchair. It had most certainly made me have wild dreams.

Thinking of them, I was again filled with bewilderment. I dream often and I can always remember them. To the last detail. Ivana has never believed me about that. Maybe because all of her dreams vanish before she wakes up. She cannot even remember if she has dreamt at all. I clearly remembered that I had dreamt last night—and it was something most unusual and long—but I couldn't manage to recall anything about it.

Knowing myself, I would remain in that uncomfortable position in the armchair until I plucked the dream from my memory, no matter how long it took, but then

I felt ashamed of myself. I had really found a bad time to defend the threatened honor of my good memory for dreams. I should have thought of Ivana immediately upon opening my eyes.

I almost leapt from the armchair, then began pacing about under the imperative to do something. Anything. I grabbed my cell phone from the desk in the faint hope that, while sleeping, I might have missed a call or a message, but there was nothing. The only thing I could do was try once again to contact Senior Inspector Mrvaljević, but she was surely sleeping now after pulling the night shift. It was only 8:37, as the clock on my phone informed me.

Sighing helplessly, I headed for the bathroom. In the dark mood that overcame me, it suddenly became important for me to free myself of the clothing in which I had spent the night, as if it were to blame for all my troubles. I remained under the shower at least twice as long as usual. As I dried my head, I thought that I heard the muffled sound coming from my study to inform me that an SMS or e-mail had arrived, but being still half wet, I did not immediately rush in there. A bit calmer now than when I had entered the bathroom, I was aware that I dare not fall into the trap spoken of in the Chinese proverb: "If you're expecting a horseman, you have to be very careful not to mistake your heartbeat for the beat of a horse's hoofs."

When I returned freshly clothed to my study, however, it turned out that it had been a horseman after all. An e-mail from Ivana was waiting for me on my phone.

WITH IMPATIENT, ALMOST FEVERISH moves, I opened the virtual envelope, overtaken by anxiety, as if I had received a verdict of some sort. However, no kind of message appeared on the telephone screen. The subject line was empty, and beneath it there were two and a half lines of some kind of link in which nothing meaningful could be deciphered: just a long, seemingly random series of large and small blue letters, numbers and various symbols.

I managed to resist the temptation to click on it immediately. For a while now, staring at the tiny screen on my mobile phone has been hard on my eyes. They tear up quickly. Perhaps the link's content was something short and easily visible, but if not, there was no reason to strain my eyes. Whatever it was, I would see it better and more comfortably on the computer monitor. That much patience I did have.

Although it did not last for even a minute, the system boot seemed to drag on forever. While it was ongoing, I turned off the e-mail notifications on my cell phone. I do so whenever I turn the computer on. I do not like receiving signals from two sources. At last, I saw on the big screen the rambling link which filled up an entire line. I hurriedly moved the cursor to it and then pressed the left mouse button, harder than necessary.

A high-resolution video appeared. I could have seen

it quite well even if I had been leaning back in my desk chair, but still, unconsciously, I moved closer to the screen. From the pair of speakers emanated sounds which I probably least expected.

When the recording finished after two minutes and fourteen seconds, I kept leaning forwards for several long moments. Then I played it again and finally leaned into the soft back of the chair. I paused the video three times to observe a scene more closely. After finishing the second playing, I remained motionless for a brief while, then picked up my telephone. I would let it ring until I woke up Senior Inspector Mrvaljević. She had some explaining to do.

She answered before the second ring.

"Good morning, Professor Živković." Her voice was not groggy.

"Good morning, Ms. Mrvaljević. I hope I have not awakened you," I said, just in case.

"You didn't wake me up. I'm working the morning shift today."

I considered for a moment whether to ask her if she had seen my missed call from the previous night, but that would just give her a chance to reprimand me for calling so late.

"I have news. Ivana has just sent me an e-mail."

"Great. Now you know first-hand that she is all right."

"She is not…"

"No?"

"Last night you told me that she was still in Serbia, did you not?"

"I did."

"Well, she is not."

"She went somewhere after we talked?"

"She would not have managed to travel so far if she had left after midnight."

"So far? Where did she contact you from?"

"From the jungle. And as far as I know, the closest jungle is at least ten hours' or so flight from Serbia. She would have had to depart a long time before midnight. You, however, told me that you had checked with customs and immigration and that…"

"You're sure she's reached some sort of jungle?" the senior inspector interrupted me.

"Quite certain. I saw Ivana in the jungle with my very own eyes. She sent me a short video. A link, in fact…"

"Could you forward it to me?"

"Gladly."

"I'll send you my e-mail address by SMS right now."

"All right."

I am very interested—I thought when she had hung up—to hear what she will have to say when she watches the video. How had Ivana managed to get through passport control undetected and board an airplane?

My phone notified me that I had a message. I opened my e-mail window on the computer and typed the address from my telephone into the "To:" line. If Ivana had been here, she would have teased me over this. She would never re-type anything from the phone, but would resort to some sort of quicker and more reliable way. However, I remain conservatively faithful to my old habits.

Having sent the link to the inspector, I watched the recording once again. I turned up the volume a little. My ears filled with the sounds of the jungle. I would have recognized them even without the images. The house where we stayed on Sri Lanka lay right on the edge of the jungle, thus we were constantly surrounded by a variety of calls from the multitude of tropical forest creatures: screeches, whistles, squawks, croaks, growls...

The view shown on the screen was quite similar to the one stretching from our balcony on the second floor in Unawatuna. The camera recording it was probably mounted on a branch of sorts. The scene was filled with a seemingly impassable intertwining of green shades. There must have been a breeze because the thick vegetation was fluttering.

For fifteen seconds, nothing happened, and then a female figure stepped into the scene from the right. From this angle, her face could not be seen, but there was no doubt about who it was. Would anyone else be dressed in such a place as Ivana had been yesterday when she went out into the Belgrade winter evening? She was wearing everything Ms. Mrvaljević had enumerated: a long gray overcoat, a dark red woolen scarf, a beret. I could not see her feet, but I did not doubt that she was wearing black ankle boots. All of it perfectly suitable for a trek through the jungle. She had a large taupe purse in her left hand while wielding a black umbrella in her right, as if clearing a path through the jungle with a machete.

It was not easy for her to penetrate the intertwined and interwoven bushes. Even though Ivana was valiantly swiping left and right, it took her more than a minute and a half to cover ten meters of ground to the left side of the screen. Finally arriving, she stopped, turned back and looked at the camera positioned high above her, as if she somehow knew that it was right there. For several moments she just smiled, then waved at me with the umbrella handle. Then she pressed on.

A second before the video was to end, I paused it and leaned towards the monitor again. Along the left edge, the leafy veil seemed a little thinner. I had not just imagined it before: there, in the midst of all the vegetation, a dark yellow blur could be seen which would have been indiscernible with a poorer resolution. As if a wall were looming nearby, towards which Ivana was heading.

9

I CLOSED THE VIDEO window, took the phone, and rose from the desk. Normally, at this time, I would go to the bakery to pick up breakfast. Today I would skip that. Instead of freshly baked bagels, I would have freshly made toast. If Senior Inspector Mrvaljević called me while I was out, it would be inappropriate for me to talk to her in front of witnesses in the bakery or in the street. Many people no longer care about such things, but I avoid phone calls in the company of others, even when the topics are harmless, much less when something as delicate as Ivana's disappearance was at stake.

I had already stepped into the kitchen when a thought occurred to me. I changed course and headed to the bedroom. I should have checked this the night before. Just in case. Ivana kept her documents in the middle one of three in the chest of drawers. Amongst the multitude of other objects, there was also a rather large leather folder. It was crammed full, but I did not have to thumb through the bundle of papers. Her passport was lying on top. There was no reason to check—whose else would it be other than Ivana's?—but still I opened it and was ashamed at my lack of confidence when I looked into her lovely eyes in the picture.

I returned the passport to the folder, but I did not shut the drawer immediately. I went on staring at the jumble of contents even though, actually, I did not see it because my thoughts were so completely occupied with hard questions.

In what magical way had Ivana managed to board an airplane without her passport yesterday? To be fair, she could enter several of the surrounding countries with just her ID card, but her departure would be registered anyway, and none of those countries had a jungle. Only one other possibility crossed my mind: Ivana had another passport about which I did not know. Perhaps she had a different surname in it. She had never married, at least as far as I knew, but truthfully speaking, I did not know much about Ivana's past. She had never expounded on her earlier relationships, nor was I curious about them. Still, if she had left Serbia under another name, she had not done so with a different face. She must have been recorded by a plethora of cameras. It was unlikely that there was a place better covered by video surveillance than the airport. I would not be surprised if they oversaw even the toilets there... If this proved to be true—and I could not see what else could be—then the inspector would have to explain why she had deceived me by claiming that Ivana was still in the country.

I finally closed the drawer and went off again to the kitchen. My stomach was now audibly demanding satisfaction.

The sudden insight that my presupposition about a second passport was not accurate disturbed the comfort of my meal. Ivana could have another surname, but not other biometric data. They would be the same in both passports, thus it would surely be known if she had left Serbia, regardless of the passport she had used. Maybe the inspector had not deceived me. What reason could she have, in any case, to do that?

However, if Ivana was still in the country, how could she send me a video from the jungle? Here I was back at square one. Seemingly, I would not be able to move further without the aid of Ms. Mrvaljević. I briefly checked the phone lying in front of me on the table. Thirteen minutes to ten. I sighed. Hopefully she would call soon.

The phone rang while I was doing the breakfast dishes in the kitchen sink. I hurriedly wiped my hands on a dishtowel, grabbed the phone, and almost shouted:

"Hello!"

"Professor Živković, I'm afraid we have a problem."

"Of course we have a problem. I have been telling you that since last night. Have you seen the video?"

"I did."

"And? What do you have to say?"

She seemed to hesitate momentarily before she answered, "Interesting…"

I waited for her to add something, but she did not go on.

"That's it? It is impossible that it just looked interesting to you."

"Why impossible?"

"Because it is impossible for Ivana to be simultaneously in Belgrade, as you claim, and in some distant jungle from which she sends me a video of herself."

"It could have been pre-recorded and sent from here today."

My countenance fell like a chess player's who has just blundered. How had I not thought of such a simple possibility? But then a comeback hit me.

"It could not have been pre-recorded. You saw how Ivana was dressed."

"Too warmly for a jungle, yes."

From her tone of voice, I would say she was smiling.

"Apart from that. The grey overcoat. She bought it this summer. At a sale. We were together. I remember it well. She kept trying it on for a long time, even by her standards. After that, she did not go abroad at all."

"Then there's got to be another explanation, because Ms. Đurić is certainly still in Belgrade. The part of town she's in is quite well covered by cameras. She hasn't left the building she entered last night. We checked carefully. There's only one exit."

I cleared my throat. "And you still will not tell me where she is?"

"I can't. I explained why. But maybe you'll draw your own conclusions if you agree to help me."

"How can I help you?"

"I would send you by SMS a list of the occupants of that building. It's not impossible that you'll recognize someone. That's the easiest way for us to get to Ms. Đurić."

I remained silent for several moments.

"I don't understand…"

"Ms. Đurić is in one of eight apartments," the senior inspector interrupted me. "Actually, seven, because one of them is unoccupied. The owners live abroad, and they don't rent it out. We can go from apartment to apartment, but that takes time, and we would be disturbing the tenants. If you recognize a name, we could try there first. That would be less intrusive."

I wished to ask several questions at once; seconds passed of my renewed silence, until finally, one question outweighed the others.

"But why are you searching for Ivana at all? What do you need her for? Last night you told me that the… case… was closed for you."

"It was closed until you e-mailed me half an hour ago. Something is wrong with... the link..."

She paused as if searching for the right words to continue.

"What is wrong? Just an ordinary link..."

"It seems to be quite extraordinary. I forwarded your e-mail to my colleagues in the Internet Crimes Division. That's standard procedure. They quickly raised an alarm. That link of Ms. Đurić's is not a link at all..."

"What is it then?" I now impatiently interrupted her.

"No one knows. That's the problem. They've never seen anything like it."

"But whatever it is, it's completely harmless. It just leads to a recording..."

"... A recording which is anything but harmless. One would say that it was made today on the other side of the world, but in it is a woman who has not stepped out of a Belgrade building since last night. My colleagues want to get in touch with her as soon as possible to clear up the ambiguities."

"And now you want me to help you get to Ivana? To participate in her arrest? Do you really believe that..."

"There will be no arrest, Professor Živković. There's no reason for it. No laws have been violated. Ms. Đurić is not suspected of anything. Just a brief informative conversation."

"No matter, I am not a stool-pigeon..."

"Of course not. But you're a sensible man who understands that something extraordinary is going on. And who himself wants to find out what happened to the woman he lives with, right?"

"Yes, but..."

"You can find that out most easily by cooperating with us. We're just asking you to check if you know anyone on a short list of the building's inhabitants. That's all." She paused, then added, "For now."

I fell silent for a third time. The senior inspector was right. I could not hope to find a trace of Ivana without the help of the police. On the other hand, she might see that as a betrayal for which she could never forgive me…

As I hesitated and Ms. Mrvaljević patiently awaited my response, the sound of a gong came from my study. It was loud enough for the inspector to hear it as well.

"Did you just get a new e-mail?" she asked, her voice slightly raised.

"Yes. The computer is on in my study…"

"If it's from Ms. Đurić, please don't open it. By no means. Give me the password to your e-mail. Quickly."

"But I do not want anyone else to have access…"

"My colleagues need fifteen minutes to figure it out themselves. By doing this, you're confirming that you're willing to cooperate. I promise you that no one will misuse it."

"If Ivana sent me a new video, I would also like to see it…"

"You'll see it, don't worry. I'll call you soon to tell you that you can freely open your e-mail. Whatever is in it."

I sighed. "All right. Here is my password: Ivana2018. Capital 'I'."

"I'll call you soon, Professor Živković," the senior inspector answered hastily as soon as she had written it down.

10

I RUSHED TO MY study, leaving the dishes unfinished.

The second e-mail also had just one long blue line of seemingly senseless letters and symbols. A new "link" which—as had just been established—was not that at all.

It was not easy to suppress my desire to click on the only writing in the e-mail and see what Ivana had sent me now. This frustration was joined by my guilty conscience. Reason told me that, actually, it was inconsequential that I had given Ms. Mrvaljević my password, because they would have got it anyway even if I hadn't started to cooperate, and there was no reason to slow them down. To the contrary. Still, I felt that, with that act, I had turned my back on Ivana.

From these dark thoughts I was roused by the arrival of the promised SMS from the senior inspector. I sat down at my desk, opened the message, and began looking over the list containing the twenty-six names of residents in the unknown building. The inspector called me just as I reached the end. She got straight down to business, professionally, without niceties.

"Do you recognize any of them?"

"No. I do not know any of these people."

"Are you sure?"

"I'm positive. I'm sorry. What will you do now—go from apartment to apartment?"

"We have no other choice."

A thought crossed my mind. "Why not try to trace Ivana's telephone? I read somewhere that a phone's location can be established even if it is turned off. The police must surely have the equipment to do so, do they not?"

"We already tried. Nothing came of it. She must have taken out the battery."

"I don't think Ivana would know how to do that, even if she wished to."

"Then she was helped by someone who does."

"But why would she remove her battery?"

"Why do people take the battery out of their phones? So they can't be traced."

"That would mean she had thought of the possibility that the police were searching for her. If she wanted to be unavailable only to me, it would be enough for her just to switch off the phone."

"She must have figured that you'd call the police because of her disappearance."

I thought about it briefly. "I know that you cannot reveal the address of the building, but if you could just tell me what part of the city she is in, perhaps I could draw conclusions based on that..."

"Please don't insist, Professor Živković."

"All right, fine. I shan't insist. However, there is something that you can certainly tell me. Something quite significant to me. It surely will not endanger your investigation."

"What is that?"

"Did Ivana meet someone last night before entering that building? I don't care who it was. It will be enough if you just answer 'yes' or 'no'."

Silence prevailed at the other end.

"We are cooperating now, correct?" I added. "And cooperation ought to work both ways, otherwise it is not cooperation…"

We passed a few more moments in silence before the inspector spoke up.

"No, Ms. Đurić didn't meet anyone before going into the building. If she had, it would be easier for us to find her now."

"Thank you!" My voice sounded more elated than I would have wished.

"You're welcome." Once again, I had the impression she was smiling.

"Did you see the new message?" I changed the subject.

"I did."

"The new video?"

"Yes."

"And? What is it like?"

"Interesting… You can also take a look."

"I can hardly wait."

"Please call me after you see it."

"Absolutely."

I put down the phone and hurriedly clicked on the so-called link. The screen instantly filled with a view of a room.

The camera was obviously above a high window because an abundance of light came from beneath. The furniture was sparse—a narrow bed with a brass frame, a white nightstand holding a lamp with a yellow shade, a tall thin chair with a low back, like a barstool. One door was on the left, and another was on the opposite wall, where three pictures were hanging. For some reason, they were covered with black cloths.

Nothing happened this time either for about fifteen

seconds and then Ivana came in through the door on the left.

She was dressed like before—in winter clothes. First she put her purse and umbrella on the chair, then she squatted down and reached for something under the bed. From there she took out a large drawing pad. A charcoal drawing stylus was attached to it. I had seen both of these objects before in artists' stores. She sat on the edge of the bed, crossed her legs, pulled up her sleeves a little, flipped over the cover of the pad, then looked up and stared at the camera. I was overcome with the strange impression that she was actually watching me attentively just then, as if this were not a recording but a live broadcast. After several moments she quickly began making broad strokes on the paper with the charcoal stylus.

When she soon looked at me again, smiling, she waved at me with the hand holding the stylus. She raised her eyes to the camera briefly once more before the recording ended. It lasted just one minute and eleven seconds.

I played the video again, then paused the picture when Ivana stepped into the room. This time I did not reflexively move my head towards the monitor, but rather magnified a section of the picture. A small part of the corridor behind her looked commonplace: a white wall, a dark red carpet.

I turned off the recording, then called the senior inspector.

"Is that room familiar to you?" she asked me as soon as we were connected.

"No."

"Are you sure?"

"I have never seen it before."

"Did you maybe notice anything connected to the previous video? Anything at all?"

"I noticed one difference. The second recording was made somewhere quite far from the first."

"How did you come to that conclusion?"

"By the bed. I have been to Sri Lanka. Right by the jungle. There, all beds have mosquito nets. A gauze netting canopy. Wherever this latter room is, it is definitely not in the tropics. Only, how did Ivana manage to go first to the jungle and then return to a temperate region in such a short time?"

"She didn't have to travel at all to send you these videos. She is still in Belgrade. That's the only thing we know without a doubt."

"What do you mean—she did not have to travel? You yourself saw her in the jungle in the first video, and I explained about the overcoat to you."

"The overcoat proves nothing. Both videos could have been made here."

"Here? Where is there a jungle in Belgrade?"

"It's unnecessary. Today, people record perfect illusions."

"Special effects? Do you know how much that costs? Where would Ivana get that kind of money? And besides, why would she spend it that way?"

"It costs almost nothing. Apps are either free or really cheap. Anyone with even a modicum of experience can produce nearly any sort of trick film with a normal cell phone."

"I had no idea…"

"One would expect a writer of fantastika to be somewhat better informed…" This she said in a lightly mocking, good-natured way.

I cleared my throat. "Fantastika and science fiction

are not the same thing. In any case, no matter, it may well be as you say; the question remains as to why Ivana would get involved in all this."

"Only Ms. Đurić can answer that one. I hope we find her soon."

"Have you inquired amongst the residents of that building?"

"It doesn't go that fast. The team has only just gone to the scene. I'll call you with any news when they finish. In the meantime, our experts are checking the first recording. They're not, however, very optimistic. They say that if it's skillfully done, it's quite difficult to determine that it's not authentic. But all this is less important. The main problem is that there has been no advance on the so-called links. Ms. Đurić has confronted us with quite a serious problem." She paused briefly. "By the way, did you happen to notice anything unusual about her? Either in the first or the second recording?"

"Unusual?"

"Anything that might seem odd about her to you."

"The jungle is certainly not usual for her…"

"I didn't mean the surroundings, but her… demeanour."

"Is there some reason for you to ask me that?"

"No. I am just curious."

I reflected for a moment, then shook my head, as if the inspector could see me. "No… I didn't notice anything unusual. Ivana seemed quite normal, even though she shouldn't because everything is far from normal."

"All right. If another e-mail comes from Ms. Đurić like the previous two—please, don't look at the video immediately. Give us at least three minutes so that we can access it first."

"Absolutely."

I put the phone down on the desk. This was not in the spirit of our newly-established cooperation. I had kept something from her. But she had also not been honest with me when she said that she was just curious. Ivana seemed to be too relaxed in the first recording, which is not like her at all. Not in a million years would she go alone deep into the jungle. Unless, of course, it was not a jungle at all, but just a special effect. In the second recording, there was also something puzzling, but it could not be explained by filmmaking tricks. She made confident, experienced movements with the stylus on paper, even though she has absolutely no talent for drawing. She would not even know how to draw a stick figure.

11

I GOT UP AND went to the kitchen to finish washing the dishes. When I was done, I had to think of something to occupy myself. If the situation were normal, I would have enjoyed most trying to write, but under these exceptional circumstances, that was not possible. I doubted that I would be focused enough to read either, even such an exciting book as Binet's. My thoughts would constantly loop back to the ever more bewildering events related to Ivana's disappearance.

Otherwise, the day was almost made for writing. On Wednesdays, I do not have classes or any other obligations. Still, to be honest, I doubted that I would have made use of these propitious circumstances even if everything had been all right with Ivana. I would, though, spend some time in front of the blank screen staring at the blinking cursor, but it is doubtful that anything would come of it.

This had been going on for almost a month. Something unusual was happening. This was no banal writer's block. After all, I had never experienced anything like it. I am not one of those writers who sits down at the computer and only then begins thinking through what they might write about. I sit down to work only when a new work has ripened in me. It already exists, formed somewhere in my unconscious, and all that is left for me is "just" to write it down.

The usual signals were now arriving from my unconscious that the critical mass had been reached and the new prose text was ready, but when I would take my place in front of the screen, it was as if an invisible barrier appeared. Nothing was coming out, even though I almost physically felt the internal pressure.

I ascribed this at first to the long break I had taken from writing prose. Five years had already passed since I had finished my last novel—*The Image Interpreter*. There had never been such a long gap between two works. I had written, to be fair, other kinds of texts in the meantime, but they did not count. One becomes unaccustomed to writing prose; it is not like swimming or riding a bicycle, where you are back in business almost immediately. I needed a little time, I consoled myself; soon enough the barrier would lower and everything would flow smoothly as always.

I waited patiently for that to happen, but barren days succeeded one another, and the barrier stood stoutly, although it seemed that the pressure was increasing. I found myself ever more frustrated because of this, and the feeling was accompanied by difficult, dire questions.

Why on earth should I delve into writing one more book? Were twenty-two not enough to say everything I had to say in prose, so that I needed a twenty-third as well? After how many books does a writer become a scribomaniac? Isn't one of the greatest authorial virtues knowing when to quit, despite the vain urge to continue writing? Not shooting yourself in the foot by writing unnecessary books in which, at best, you just keep repeating yourself?

It turned out that Ivana's disappearance actually had the tiniest of upsides. It gave me a justification, at least today, for avoiding confrontation with these somber issues. My conscience stung me because of such thoughts, but not too much. It was understanding of my secret vexations.

Very well, I would not write or read, but what should I do with myself while I waited? Perhaps I could go out for a walk where there were not many people around? I could take my phone with me so I would not miss a single e-mail or call from the inspector, and it would soothe me to move about and take in some fresh winter air. But then again—no, it would not be appropriate for me to walk around while a multitude of policemen were searching for Ivana. I had to stay home.

As I stood there by the kitchen sink, a dishtowel still in hand, not knowing what else to do, a new gong sounded in my study, as if coming to my aid. I laid the towel aside and hastened there. Just as I reached my desk, my telephone rang.

"Just to remind you: wait a while before you open the new e-mail," the senior inspector said, as if apologizing.

"Not to worry. I can restrain myself when necessary."

"A new problem has arisen. Have you tried to watch either of the two videos again?"

"I have not."

"Could you try? Just be careful not to touch the third one yet."

"I'll be careful. You have so little confidence in me…"

"I do have confidence in you. It's just that everyone makes mistakes."

I sighed, then clicked on the "link" in Ivana's first e-mail. I pressed the mouse button several more times. Nothing happened. It was the same with the second e-mail.

"They don't work anymore."

"We hoped that maybe they had remained active on your computer."

"How could they be active on my computer and not on yours?"

"Normally they couldn't be. But it seems that here nothing is normal."

"Did you save the videos?"

"We didn't manage to record them. There wasn't enough time to hack the protections."

"I thought you had good experts."

"We do. There are also better ones. If need be, we can call them in to help us too."

I hesitated briefly. "The National Security Agency?"

"You can watch the third video now, Professor Živković," she circumvented the question. "We'll talk soon."

12

RECORDED FROM OVERHEAD, A large desk filled the monitor. It stood next to a wide window with the shutters down almost two-thirds of the way. It was enough for the sun's rays, which penetrated in bright beams, not to bother the person sitting in the high-backed chair, while still amply accenting the octagonal crystal dish set in the centre of the window sill. The bowl, most likely, was originally an aquarium—I had seen similar ones in pet stores—but now it served as a flower pot for a collection of miniature cacti, with white and pink artificial blossoms.

It was not difficult to imagine that the scene on the screen was part of someone's study. Not necessarily that of a writer, though that would be the most likely. I judged by myself. I would have enjoyed working in such an ambience. Its attractiveness was enhanced, also, by the light seeping in through the thin slats of the Venetian blinds, creating shimmering arabesques in the dusky air of the room.

A large monitor occupied the center of the dark brown desk. To the right of it stood a black printer. Of the same color were the keyboard, mouse, and horizontally-placed computer case to the left. Everything was symmetrically arranged, almost down to the inch, with nothing out of place. A truly orderly person worked here.

Ivana emerged from the invisible area in front of the desk. She was dressed as before. She placed her free hand on the back of the chair, turned towards the camera, smiled, and then sat down. She set her purse in front of the printer and hung her umbrella from the edge of the desk.

She remained motionless for several moments. I was watching her from behind so I could not see her facial expression. Then she pushed her interwoven fingers out before her, turned her palms towards the window and stretched. When she jiggled the mouse, the screen went blank white. She moved her hands towards the keyboard, paused for a moment, then began feverishly typing like a pianist playing *presto*. The music of the keys filled the silence of the room. It did not last long.

The video was the shortest of the three: just forty-eight seconds. I did not have to watch it again. I had already noticed something unusual. Apparently, Ivana had become a professional typist overnight. Until just yesterday, she had typed with two fingers, which was, to be fair, twice as fast as I type because I do so only with my right index finger.

My cell phone rang just as I finished the video.

"Do you recognize anything?" Senior Inspector Mrvaljević asked me. A hint of impatience could be heard in her voice.

"No. I have never seen this desk. Or the window."

"What kind of desk does Ms. Đurić have?"

"Different. Smaller. All in lively colors." I paused for a moment. "And it is all messy…"

"And yours?"

"Mine is much more orderly."

The inspector seemed to consider briefly whether to comment on this, but then changed the subject.

"Our forensic team should come and visit your place as soon as possible."

"Forensic team? Goodness, no one has been killed…" A sudden thought took my breath away. "Right?" I added softly.

"No, of course not. Forensics doesn't deal only with homicide."

"In TV series…"

"Real police work is rather different from what you see in TV series."

"What could interest forensics experts here?"

"Clues to Ms. Đurić. Your home is the only place where they exist for certain."

"What kind of clues?"

"Any kind. Anything that could help us get on her trail."

"Get on her trail?" I repeated, perplexed. "Why would you get on her trail? I mean, you know where she is—in the building she entered last night and never left. You made that claim yourself. All that remains is for you to establish which apartment she is in. Have you ascertained that?"

"We have established that she is not located in seven of the apartments. There is still the eighth one where no one is living. We'll try to contact the owners who are in America, as soon as it's morning there. We need their permission to enter."

"How could Ivana be in the apartment of strangers who are in America?"

"Maybe she knows them. Checks their apartment from time to time. It's not so unusual."

"She never told me that she was apartment-sitting for anyone. What is their surname?"

"Nišavić."

"She never mentioned anyone by the name of Nišavić. I would remember it, it is a rare last name. All of this seems most improbable to me."

"On the contrary, it's much more probable than these messages you are getting from Ms. Đurić."

"And what if you don't manage to contact the owners, or if they don't give you permission?"

"We'll get a warrant to search the apartment. We've already requested one. Just in case."

"But if it is established that Ivana is not in that eighth apartment either?"

She did not answer immediately. I heard her give a sigh.

"Well, that would be extremely improbable. But not impossible either. That is the very reason we now want to gather clues about Ms. Đurić at your place, in the unlikely event that she is also not in the eighth apartment. So we don't lose time. If we don't find her there, we'll step up the investigation…"

"That is out of the question!" I interrupted her and did not even attempt to dilute my angry tone. "I shall not allow you to fumble through Ivana's things as if she were a common criminal. You cannot expect me to cooperate to such an extent."

"We can also carry out a search without your approval. We can easily get a warrant for that too. Only that wouldn't be good for you. You would fall under suspicion of being in cahoots with Ms. Đurić, of being her co-conspirator."

"Conspirator—in what? What has Ivana done wrong apart from sending some sort of unusual links? In all of this, she is a victim, not a perpetrator."

"The links are so unusual they've caught the attention of the National Security Agency. Trust me, it's better for you to cooperate with us. They have a completely different understanding of cooperation."

We spent several moments in silence, and then I too sighed. "All right, send in the forensics team. Do they need my help in any way?"

"No. Actually, it would be best if you weren't even there while they worked. They won't stay long, half an hour at most. Why don't you go for a walk? I'll call you as soon as they're finished."

"I hope they won't make a mess…"

"Not to worry. You won't even know they've been there."

"I'll wait for them to let them in and give them a spare key to the apartment. They can just put it in my mailbox when they leave."

"Just go ahead and leave immediately. Don't worry about unlocking and locking the apartment. Everything will be just fine."

13

THE SOUND OF A notification interrupted me while ty-
ing my left shoelace. Reflexively I started to straighten
up, but then I remembered that there was actually no
reason to hurry. If a new e-mail had arrived from Ivana, I would have to wait for the police to watch it first,
and I was not interested in other e-mails right now. I
continued lacing up my winter boots.

Ivana's fourth message did not differ from the first
three: a long series of blue letters, numbers, and symbols without any particular order. I had no idea where
she was getting these mysterious links which were not
links at all, and which had aroused the interest of even
the National Security Agency. Ivana is more competent
in the digital world than I am—which is not saying
much—but this was something far beyond her pur-
view. Someone must be helping her, someone quite
skillful and self-confident, since they had decided to
outsmart the police. I was intrigued, of course, about
who that person might be, but even more so about the
meaning of all this. What was Ivana trying to achieve?
And why?

I was roused from my ruminations by a new SMS.
The inspector had written just one word: *Watch.*

As I reached for the mouse, I wondered how she knew
I was still at home. Then it occurred to me: through a
surveillance camera somewhere nearby. In the record-

ings from that camera, she had seen Ivana leaving the building the night before at five-thirty and heading to some place in town still unknown to me.

I shook my head, then clicked on the "link".

Again there was the scene of a room shot from above. It was rather large, with three high windows covered with thick dark drapes. In the middle of the uncarpeted floor were five comfortable armchairs, arranged in a semicircle. Beside each was a small table with a bottle of sparkling water, an inverted glass on a napkin, and a white folder. In front of the chairs was an easel covered with black velvet. A spotlight on the ceiling was aimed at it. There was no other lighting. The corners of the room were in semi-darkness.

Everything was still for about ten seconds, then Ivana entered through a large double door on the left. As if someone invisible had opened it for her from the outside. She was dressed as before. She approached the middle chair in the semicircle and sat down. On the chair to her left she put her purse and umbrella, her beret on the right one, then shook out her hair by tossing her head.

She opened a bottle of mineral water, filled a glass to the top, then drank the whole thing down. She seemed to be quite thirsty. Next she picked up a folder, took out a stack of large photographs and started browsing through them. After the fourth, she looked up at the camera. A smile spread across her face as she shook her right index finger at me, as if she were scolding me for something she had seen in the picture. Then she took a pen from her purse, turned the photograph over, put it on the little table, and wrote something on the back.

She returned the photograph to the folder, the pen to her purse, then got up. She approached the easel and stood before it. After a brief hesitation she prudently took hold of the edge of the velvet cover and first lifted it slightly, as if something might jump out from under it. Since nothing did, she lifted the dark red drape under which, on a small lectern, stood a book, apparently antique. She looked it over curiously, still not daring to touch it. Eventually, she mustered up the courage: she gently picked up the hefty tome in both hands, as if it might fall apart otherwise.

She returned to the middle chair, opened the book and delved into it, transforming into a statue. This renewed stasis lasted as long as that at the beginning, and then the video ended. The chronometer at the bottom of the screen showed one minute and twenty-four seconds.

Even had I had the chance to watch the video again, I would not have needed to. It had not escaped me that Ivana had written something on the back of the photo with her left hand, although she is right-handed.

I closed the video window and returned to the hallway. I put on my overcoat, wrapped around my neck a long brick-red woolen scarf that Ivana had bought me for my last birthday, and pulled on my gloves. The tip of the index finger was missing on the right glove, so that I could use the cell phone while I was wearing them. I put on a dark brown leather cap, but did not go out immediately. I re-entered the living room and looked around. I was sorry that I had given permission for strangers to crowd in here, freely digging into the intimate world of Ivana and myself. But there was no going back.

Stopping at the front door, I wondered for a moment whether to lock it or not. On second thought, I could actually have left it wide open as a sign of welcome.

The forensics team was about to arrive. Locks like mine were obviously no barrier to them, but why should they be detained even briefly by opening it with a skeleton key or some other tool of theirs? Nevertheless, I turned the key in the lock. Twice. I had indeed become a police collaborator, but not of my own free will. Let them struggle a little bit.

14

THE BRIGHT BITING SUN made me squint when I stepped out of the building. It was colder than I'd expected. The frost immediately pinched my cheeks, and my breath emerged as steam. I turned my overcoat collar up over my scarf and headed towards Mihajlo Pupin Boulevard where I usually walk.

Passing by a lamppost, I began wondering where the surveillance cameras were located. I had never noticed a single one before, nor had I heard anyone mention them, but that, I guess, is the way it should be. What kind of surveillance would it be if everyone knew from where they were being watched?

I had already reached the short flight of steps that leads down to the Boulevard when something crossed my mind. I stopped at the first step, turned in the direction from which I had come, and raised my left foot to the upper level. I leaned over and started to fiddle with my shoelace. First I untied and loosened it, then slowly began to tighten and tie it. From time to time, I would unobtrusively look towards the entranceway to my building.

At least, I thought it was unobtrusive, until my cell phone rang.

"You won't see them, Professor Živković," said the senior inspector. "They are already in your apartment. They went in through the garage entrance."

I felt like a naïve little kid caught in some sort of mischief. Not knowing what to say, I just cleared my throat, straightened up, and continued down the steps with the phone to my ear. I stopped when I stepped onto the Boulevard and looked first in one direction, then the other. This, it seemed, caused the inspector to think I was wondering which way to go.

"To the left, please," she said.

I indicated that direction with my free hand.

"Yes."

I shrugged, then turned left along the wide sidewalk, beside the row of oaks with their bare winter branches. In the otherwise busy street, there was almost no one.

I took a few steps, then asked, "Is there some reason for me to go in this direction?"

"The camera coverage is better there."

I nodded, satisfied by the answer. Honest and with no circumspection. As good cooperation ought to be.

"Would you tell me, Professor Živković, is everything all right between you and Ms. Đurić?"

"In what sense?"

"Have there been any... misunderstandings... arguments... between the two of you? Anything that might make her leave the place... leave you?"

"Why do you think she has left me? Ivana has gone missing. Something has happened to her. If you had started searching for her last night, when I reported her disappearance, you might have found her by now. And you are still hesitating to find out if she is in that eighth apartment. You are waiting for the owners on the other side of the world to wake up. If your forensic team can effortlessly enter a locked apartment and leave no trace of themselves behind, as you yourself told me they could, then why not do that at the Nišavić apartment?"

"We have to obey the law. With an illegal entry into that apartment, nothing we found could be used as material evidence. Just be patient a little longer. We'll go in there soon, with the owners' permission or a search warrant, it doesn't matter."

"And what if it is too late? If something… happens to her… in the meantime?"

"Nothing will happen to her. If she were in any sort of danger, would she be doing these things? Ms. Đurić does not fit at all into the missing person's profile. Such people vanish without a trace because that's their intention, or whoever is behind their disappearance quickly appears with some sort of demand. Here, however, we have something completely atypical. Ms. Đurić seems to disappear, then begins sending you enigmatic video messages via even more enigmatic links, not caring at all if she draws the attention of the police. She's certainly not doing so for no reason. Why couldn't she just tell you what she wants in a simpler fashion? Why did she have to resort to something so complex? That's why I asked you if everything was all right between you."

I did not reply straight away. I nodded a greeting to my neighbor who was returning from a walk with his excessively obese Belgian shepherd, which was dragging him by the leash. He smiled at me as if apologizing for the dog.

"Everything is all right. Ivana and I have never argued, if that's what you mean. We don't always agree, of course, but there has never been cause for even the slightest argument. I concur, it's not always easy to live with a writer, it probably seemed to her now and then that I wasn't paying enough attention to her—you yourself noticed that I don't remember how she is dressed—but she could tell me anything she wanted without hesitation."

"What do you make of the four messages you've gotten?"

"I do not understand them whatsoever. The jungle could be the one on Sri Lanka, but also any other. All jungles look alike. I have never seen any of the three rooms. Nothing that Ivana is doing in them tells me anything. If she is really attempting to tell me something in the videos, I am completely in the dark. I don't see anything."

"Maybe you'll start figuring out a meaning when the new messages come."

"You think there will be more of them?"

"It would be senseless if this was it and you still don't understand it."

I did not know how to reply, so there was a brief silence.

"Speak of the devil..." the inspector spoke first. "Do you get e-mails on your cell phone?"

"Yes."

"A new message has just arrived from Ms. Đurić. Please don't open it without my approval. Put your phone back in your pocket and just keep walking in the same direction. I have to go now. I will call you again as soon as I can."

I obediently did as I was told.

I felt strangely vulnerable as I walked along the almost empty sidewalk, aware that invisible electronic eyes were monitoring my every movement. There was no sense in me trying something. Just to be caught red-handed again as I had been a few minutes earlier. And anyway, what was it I could do? Try, unnoticed, to edge the cell phone slightly out of my pocket, light up the screen and see what I almost surely already knew—that Ivana's fifth e-mail was also a false link that acted like a real one? With my hands buried in my pockets, I continued to go further from home, walking aimlessly. The cold was slowly seeping into my bones even though I was warmly dressed.

I had not deceived the inspector when I told her that I did not see any connection between the four recordings. The only common factor in them was Ivana, but she, actually, did not belong there, she was a visitor. The surroundings were all unfamiliar.

I felt as if I were in one of those television game shows where the players gradually receive clues regarding some unknown object, starting with the most indefinite. If Ivana were in my place, maybe she would already have figured something out. Sometimes we watch such a show and she generally identifies the hidden object long before me, usually by the third or fourth clue. Or even earlier. It has happened that only by the ninth or tenth, last, clue do I finally discern what the object is. If at all.

I had no idea what it was that Ivana was intending to tell me with everything that had happened since the night before, but I had a hunch that she was counting on my mediocre associative abilities. Did this "game show" of hers also have ten levels, and would I again make a fool of myself by not comprehending what she was telling me, even after the last clue was given? That would be truly shameful for a writer who prides himself on conjuring up inscrutable plots in his detective stories. What had I done wrong for her to punish me so publicly?

I had not mentioned to the inspector the single common factor that I had noticed in all four videos: tiny deviations in some of Ivana's traits—that she hates the jungle, that she types with just two fingers, that she is not skillful at drawing, and that she is right-handed. This could all easily be a misdirection. Ivana liked that narrative technique in my books, and now she had resolved to play with it a bit herself. If I had brought it to the attention of Ms. Mrvaljević, it might have sent her down the wrong path. For now, it was better not to say anything; I could do that later. Anyway, I was convinced that the police were not telling me everything either.

Buried in my contemplations, I reached the crossroads where I would have to decide which way to go. I had just begun to look around in search of one of the cameras, so I could ask by gesture for directions from the inspector, when an SMS arrived—equally as expansive as the last one: *Watch.*

To my left extended a large park. I could see no one in it. I went to the nearest bench and sat on its edge. I would not be conspicuous there. None of the still rare passers-by were likely to pay any attention to me. And what if they did? They would see a hardly unusual sight: an elderly gentleman preoccupied with his cell phone. I hurriedly pulled out the phone, took off my glasses, and held the screen close to my eyes so that I could see it as well as possible.

15

THIS TIME, THE ROOM looked like the office of some sort of high-ranking government official. The camera was located in the middle of one of the walls, just beneath the ceiling. To the right was a massive black desk. A lamp with an arched neck and green shade threw light upon a series of commonplace, symmetrically arranged objects there, amongst which was also a white flowerpot containing a bloomless plant with long narrow leaves.

Across from the desk were two massive brown leather armchairs, with a small round coffee table between them. On that table, there was a lamp with a yellow shade skirted with a fringe. Behind the chairs, shelves filled the entire wall. The books on them were of uniform height and thickness, with spines only in a few darker shades. A vertical ladder rose along the edge of the bookshelves, its ends firmly anchored to guide-rails on the floor and ceiling.

The central place on the wall across from the camera was occupied by a twin window, filled with blue sky. To the right of the window stood a pendulum clock in a tall mahogany case. To the left, next to the bookshelves, was a door of the same color as the wall, so it could be discerned only by its edges, which appeared somewhat darker.

As before, everything was briefly motionless, as if it

were a photograph and not a video, only to have Ivana's appearance give life to the scene. She came in through the inconspicuous door, still dressed the same. She first looked up at the camera and waved at me with a smile.

After that, she turned off the yellow lamp on the coffee table and the green one on the desk, then went over to the window. She struggled a little to turn the handle in the middle. When she opened it wide, a draught blew in. She retreated half a step, and her hair wisped back. Quickly, the stream of air weakened, and she went all the way to the window and leaned outwards. She put the fingers of her right hand to her lips and gave a long and piercing whistle.

She backed away. When it started happening, I had to bring the telephone closer to my face so I could better discern the colorful dots that began to fly through the window into the office from below. Butterflies! They poured in *en masse*, countless numbers of them, circling around Ivana. They surrounded her ever more densely.

When an opaque, fluttering, colorful cylinder had formed around her, a new whistle was heard, this time muffled and short. As if on command, the butterflies whisked away in harmony. It all happened in the wink of an eye. When the last of the tiny wings vanished beneath the lower edge of the window, there was no one standing in the place where Ivana had once been.

As if the draught had begun to blow again, the window slammed shut, and the handle returned to its original position. The chronometer stopped at fifty-eight seconds.

I was in despair because I would not have the chance to watch the whole thing again on a monitor. Or even on a television screen. But not so would I reveal what was wrong with Ivana this time. This I already knew. She has no idea how to whistle.

As I closed the video app, my phone began to ring. I fumbled with the phone a while before answering the senior inspector.

"Can such tricks be produced by amateurs?" I inquired without introduction.

"They can, but probably this has not been done by amateurs."

"Rather?"

"It's fairly professional…"

"Professional? But I already told you—Ivana is not in a situation to afford expensive professionals for the sake of… child's play."

"This isn't any sort of child's play, Professor Živković, but something far more serious."

"What?" I asked, perplexed.

"We still don't know. Whatever it is, it's becoming ever more complex. We entered the Nišavić apartment. We didn't manage to contact them, but we had a warrant."

"And?"

"There's no one there."

"What do you mean? Where is Ivana then? Last night you said that she had entered that building, and that she had not left…"

"That I still claim. She went into the building last night and never came out through the same door. In the eighth apartment we found traces that someone had stayed there. Once we compare them with what we found at your place, it will tell us whether it was Ms. Đurić. We're working on that already. By the way, the forensics team is finished at your apartment. You can go home. You must be freezing. It's pretty cold today—minus nine degrees."

In my excitement, I had completely forgotten about the cold. I was shaking as I rose from the bench. I returned to the Boulevard and headed off to the right with long strides.

"But if Ivana is not at the Nišavić place and has not left the building, what happened to her?"

"We were convinced that there is only one exit, but since then, we've checked again; it turns out we missed an opening at the back of the building where things are unloaded straight into the basement. The superintendent claims it was padlocked, but we didn't find a lock on the covering. Whoever knew about that opening could enter and leave the building unnoticed through it."

"How would Ivana know something like that, even presupposing that she actually did visit the Nišavić place? And why would she leave the building that way?"

"The second question is easier to answer: to go unnoticed."

"Why would she want to go unnoticed? She isn't some sort of criminal. In any case, one cannot stay unnoticed in the face of your video surveillance. Fair enough, perhaps you don't have cameras behind every single building, but you would notice as soon as she poked her nose out of such a... blind spot."

"The trouble is, she didn't poke her nose out, and she didn't stay in the blind spot."

"How can that be?"

"Our video surveillance is not perfect, unfortunately. Remember when I asked you to go walking to the left because the coverage is better there. If you had turned right and wanted to stay invisible, you could have avoided the cameras by going from one blind spot to the next."

"But how could I avoid the cameras when I didn't manage to see even one of them?"

"By accident."

"Such an 'accident' would be most improbable."

"That's true. However, there is another way to avoid the cameras. Not accidental in the least. If you know exactly where the blind spots are."

"How could anyone know that except the police?"

"That's exactly what we're wondering in the case of Ms. Đurić. There's not a trace of her on the recordings from the cameras nearest to the rear of the building. Perhaps she was incredibly lucky to accidentally move only through the blind spots. But perhaps she somehow knew where they were."

"What do you mean—'somehow'? We keep coming back to that same question."

"It's a hard question. We don't know the answer. We're investigating all possibilities."

"What possibilities?"

"She could, for instance, have found out the location of the blind spots from someone who knows about them."

I remained silent for several moments.

"Do you mean to say that someone in the police informed Ivana of the blind spots in the video surveillance? Why, that is ludicrous. Ivana does not know anyone working for the police. And even if she did, what policeman in his right mind would reveal something like that to her?"

"I agree, it isn't highly likely. Still, we're checking. But if it turns out that it wasn't an inside job, then she had help from the outside."

"The outside?"

"Yes. From someone who is a real magician, if they

managed to infiltrate the impenetrable police system. Not to mention the so-called links which are still giving us an enormous headache."

"But the chance of Ivana knowing such a magician is even less than her knowing a policeman."

"Then only one possibility remains. She's doing this all by herself, with no one to help her."

"Impossible. If you knew Ivana, such a thing would never cross your mind."

"The question, actually, is how well you know Ms. Đurić. Whatever the case, we no longer know where she is. We have put out a warrant for her arrest."

"You cannot…" I was about to object, but she interrupted me.

"There, you've reached home. Please stay there. We'll talk soon."

16

I turned the key in the lock. When I tried again, it would not turn. My uninvited guests had only locked the door once when leaving. Most likely intentionally, as a response to my locking it twice unnecessarily. I entered, locked the door behind me, took out the key and put it on the shoe cabinet, like I always do when Ivana is not home, so that she can unlock the door with her own key when she returns.

It felt really nice to be back where it was warm. I hung my scarf and overcoat on the coat rack by the front door, took off my shoes, and immediately started searching the place. I went through all the rooms, looking at everything in detail. I am one of those pedants who know not only where things are, but what position they are kept in. Ivana, who much appreciates that which she calls "creative disorder", found my excessive orderliness to be flabbergasting. She never openly objected to it, but we fought a low-intensity war over it without words. I straightened up her areas, she made a mess of mine. The main places of conflict were our desks. She would snort when she saw her desk perfectly arranged, while I would growl at the sight of chaos on mine.

I did not know what the forensics team had done over the last half hour, but at first glance, everything seemed to be entirely in order. At least on the outside.

Then it occurred to me to look inside things as well. I checked the closets, drawers, chests of drawers, display cases, shoe cabinet, looked into the laundry basket, and even—not knowing why myself—into the toilet bowl. I did not find anything unusual at all.

Scenes from spy films came to mind. Teams of technicians enter an apartment and in minutes set up surveillance and listening devices in unexpected places. I peeked into the lamps, examined the home phone, pulled the face plates off the electrical sockets, felt all around the air conditioner, shook out the cooking hood filter, opened up the remote controls. Nothing. In the end, I remembered the first thing I should have thought of. I took the little camera off the monitor, pulled its plug out of the computer housing and put it in the drawer with the other technological paraphernalia.

Standing by my desk, I slowly scanned the room, wondering where else I could look, when my phone rang.

"You might as well give up," said the inspector. "You won't find anything."

"How do you know I am even trying?" I asked after a brief hesitation.

"Firsthand. I can see you."

Frustrated, I began to look all around the room.

"Even if you looked in the right place, you wouldn't see the camera."

"How dare you!" I cried. "You have no right…" My voice broke in excitement.

"We do. We got a search warrant to carry out surveillance on your apartment while the investigation is ongoing."

"But I am not under investigation. I'm cooperating with you."

I no longer had privacy even in my own home. And it was all legal. Actually, I was supposed to be thankful because I no longer had to report Ivana. It was enough just for me to pretend that I knew nothing. How awful.

Who knows how many cameras they had put up. And where. I dared not depend on their consideration. Nothing would stop them from observing me in my bedroom. Or even in my bathroom. If only I could go looking for the cameras, regardless of the fact that the inspector thought I would uncover nothing. But if I were to try, they would see everything, and then they could accuse me of interfering with a police investigation. Anyway, even if I did manage to find them, what use would it be to me knowing where they were? I would just be tempted to remove them, and that would only make matters worse.

I opened the e-mail window and stared blankly at Ivana's six e-mails. They filled me with frustration and helplessness. When the inspector's SMS approval to watch it arrived soon thereafter, I didn't immediately click on the "link". I was suddenly overwhelmed by the childish wish to announce that I was giving up, that I would play no more, that I did not care for this game at all, they should go on without me, I was going home. But I was already at home, and the cameras were observing my every movement. In a moment or two, a female voice would encourage me to continue, there was no giving up in this game, regardless of the fact that I had not agreed to participate in the first place. Even if unwillingly, I had joined the dance, and there was no leaving it until the end.

Sighing, I clicked on the long series of various symbols.

The slanting ceiling revealed that the tiny room was

a garret. It was humbly furnished: a simple table and four chairs, a single bed, a washstand with a basin and pitcher in the corner, a large mirror. There were no rugs on the floor, no curtains at the window, no pictures on the walls. On the table lay a black violin case.

Ivana entered about ten seconds after the recording started. She approached the bed and put her umbrella and purse on it. She turned to the table, opened the case, and gracefully, as if lifting a child from a crib, picked up the violin with both hands. She held it to her bosom, admiring it. Then she looked up towards the camera in the center of the upper edge of the ceiling and nodded her head with a smile, as if confirming to me that this was exactly what she was hoping for.

Then she gently took the violin by the neck with her left hand, went to the window and opened it wide. Taking one of the chairs by its back, she moved it to the window. She retrieved the bow from the case, went to the chair, and climbed up on it without holding on. She lifted the violin to her chin and laid the bow on it. She remained motionless in that position for a few moments, gazing through the window, then started to play.

My spine began tingling. From the strings, as if from the heavens, an enchanting melody began to flow in waves. Those were the most pleasing sounds I had ever heard. My elation was mixed with disbelief. Ivana adores music and sings beautifully, but she does not play a single instrument. And only a true virtuoso could play the violin like this. The composition sounded familiar to me but, even though I struggled, I did not manage to place it, which was strange in itself because I have a good memory for music. The tempo was fast, and it grew faster. Ivana rocked the bow ever more fervently, remarkably maintaining her balance on the unsteady chair.

When the crescendo reached its peak, the violinist suddenly raised her arms in front of her, opened her hands, and let the violin and bow go. Then she spread her arms sideways, as if she were on an invisible crucifix, and began leaning forwards with her whole body, pushing her shins against the back of the chair.

The video stopped at one minute and thirty-seven seconds. If it had gone on for another moment, it would have shown whether Ivana dove through the window or flew away from it. There was no turning back.

17

THE INSPECTOR CALLED AS soon as the recording ended. She no longer had to guess when to call by the
length of the recording. She could see it all clearly.

"You could tell me where you hid the cameras. Since
you've already told me you're watching, isn't it moot
where you are doing it from? I feel silly like this: I don't
know where to look. Perhaps I have turned my back
on a lady."

"If it were so, the lady wouldn't object. Just go on as
you are. Right now I have much bigger worries than
whether my conversation partners have turned their
backs on me. The musicianship of Ms. Đurić, for example."

"Why does that worry you?"

"You don't have a violin at your place. On the Internet, nothing can be found which would connect her
with that instrument. And yet she plays like a professional. A top one, too. How do you explain that?"

"Simply. It is also a trick. A special effect. Like the
jungle or the butterflies. Ivana was only pretending to
play. We were listening to the recording of a famous
musician."

"If only the simplest explanations were always the
right ones. Have you ever held a violin?"

I reflected for a moment. "Only a toy. When I was
a child."

"I mean the real instrument. If you were to hold one, it would immediately be apparent whether you had experience with it or not. Ms. Đurić held the violin like a thoroughly accomplished violinist. That can't be faked with any sort of trickery. And then, more importantly, there was the composition itself. How did it sound to you?"

"Familiar, but I could not recognize it."

"And you couldn't have. It's not in a single music database. It was impossible to use someone else's recording because no such recording exists. Only one possibility remains: Ms. Đurić personally played a composition that she'd composed herself."

"No way. I certainly know that much about the woman I am living with. Ivana is by no means a violinist, far less a composer. You said it yourself—we don't have a violin in the apartment, and there would have to be some sort of trace of her musical career on the Internet."

"You've only been living with Ms. Đurić for the last two years. How much do you know about her previous life? That's almost half a century."

"I know very little, true. I wasn't overly inquisitive, I let her tell me whatever she wanted to. But why would she hide from me that she is a composer and a violin virtuoso? That's not some sort of stain on her past, rather something to be proud of."

"There must be a reason. Otherwise, this latest video would be impossible. Everything that's happening must be somehow related to Ms. Đurić's past. And you still can't make sense of her appearance in these various rooms? No sort of thread which would tie the six episodes together?"

"Five," I corrected her. "In the first she was in the jungle, not a room."

"Not necessarily. It could also have been recorded inside, without special effects. At the Botanical Gardens. They have a large hall with tropical vegetation."

"I hadn't thought of that."

"That possibility just occurred to us. We sent a team to check it out. So?"

I sighed. "No, I don't recognize them. I was never in a single one of those rooms. They are *terra incognita* for me."

"Maybe Ms. Đurić mentioned them earlier, alluded to them somehow…"

"If she did, I do not recall."

"Her demeanour still seems as usual?"

"Quite," I lied without hesitation. Ivana is afraid of heights. On a shaky chair, she would be overtaken by vertigo. Especially next to an open window in a garret. Not to mention leaning out…

"We're stuck," the inspector said after a short pause. "In fact, it's even worse. We have a new problem. The traces we found at the Nišavić apartment are not those of Ms. Đurić. Someone else was staying there not long ago."

"Who?"

"We still don't know. Whoever it was, they're not part of our evidence. All indications are that it was the person who looks after the apartment."

"But what happened to Ivana then?"

"She could have spent the night in one of the other seven apartments…"

"But you checked them…" I broke in.

"Yes, we did. And we're checking them again. More thoroughly."

"And if it turns out she did not…?"

"Then she left through the opening in the basement.

Probably soon after she entered the building last night. She had no reason to stay there. She just wanted to cover her tracks. To make us think she spent the night in the building."

"And she spent it—where?"

"I would love to be able to say, Professor Živković. This time, I would have no reason not to answer you. I still don't know, unfortunately, but I'll tell you as soon as I find out."

I did not manage to praise her for this exemplary cooperation on her part because she suddenly said in a frenzied voice, "Just a moment. Stay on the line."

As I was waiting, Ivana's seventh message appeared on the screen before me, with the sound of the gong.

When, a moment later, the inspector came back on, I cut her short, "Don't worry, I won't touch anything until you give the go-ahead."

"I know you won't. That's not important now. We've found Ms. Đurić. She was just caught on one of our cameras."

The inspector hung up before I had chance to ask her any of the questions that occured to me simultaneously. Did Ivana look all right? Was she alone? What was she doing? Where did they see her? Might I see the recording? Overcome with excitement, I almost jumped out of my chair. I did not care that they could see me. I grew restless in my desire to do something; I could not just go on sitting there. I headed for the front door, but stopped after two steps. It wasn't because the inspector had told me not to go anywhere. I didn't know where I would go, and it was useless to call her and insist that she tell me where Ivana was. She probably wouldn't even answer my call.

Instead of going outside, I went to the kitchen, just

to change my surroundings. They had surely hidden a camera here, too, I thought. I looked around briefly, but I saw nothing, of course. Even more frustrated, I returned to my study. I sat at the desk, put my cell phone beneath the monitor, then clicked on the "link", not caring if I had given them enough time to see the new message first.

The sixth room looked like the previous one. It was, in fact, a humble one-room apartment: a vestibule and a kitchenette could also be seen, and behind the only other door besides the front one there must have been a bathroom. Along with the table and four chairs, there was a double-fronted wardrobe, a bed, a chest of drawers, and a nightstand.

This time, Ivana announced her arrival with a short ring at the door. She entered, hung her umbrella on the coat rack in the hallway, stepped into the little room, put her bag on the table, and went into the bathroom. She stayed there for about half a minute. Since she had left the door ajar, a stream of water could be heard, probably in the sink.

After coming back in, she looked at the camera placed above the wardrobe, and smilingly showed me her hands were clean. It was only when she began to take out books that I noticed something I had missed before: her purse was quite full.

Four identical volumes were stacked on the table, and her purse had deflated like a football. The books were thick, ochre-colored hardbacks. The titles could not be read. She picked up the topmost volume, walked to the far left corner of the room, squatted down and put it right next to the corner of two walls.

She did the same with the remaining three corners.

Having done this, she stood in the center of the

room, inspected one corner after another, and nodded her head in satisfaction. She returned to the bathroom, again leaving the door ajar. The sound which soon came from there filled me with disbelief. Ivana would never shower in someone else's bathroom with the door unclosed.

The video stopped at one minute and forty-six seconds.

18

THERE WAS NO CALL from Ms. Mrvaljević. My cell phone usually rang as soon as the latest video was over, but this time no sound disturbed the quiet of my study. I continued sitting, staring at the frozen final scene on the monitor.

It was not difficult to figure out why the inspector was not calling. She was surely helping bring Ivana in for their informative conversation. Rather, to put it without obfuscation, for her arrest and interrogation. I only hoped that Ivana would not do something imprudent now. The police can be rough during an arrest, even if there is no call for it, especially towards those they have taken offense at. And they thought that Ivana had been pulling their leg since the night before.

It was a fortunate circumstance that she would be arrested in a public place, so the police would have to restrain themselves. Someone might record them. Yet Ivana dared not resist or provoke them. She had done what she had done, it remained to be seen what and why, but now it was best if she surrendered quietly, and immediately, before saying anything, asked for a lawyer. Not just because the police would avoid being violent towards her in his presence, but also because they still needed to establish whether she had actually done anything illegal.

I was still not clear what accusations they could level at

her. It was not known where she had spent the night? If that was, as I had been told the previous evening, none of her partner's business, it was even less so that of the police. She was moving around so that she could not be constantly followed by surveillance cameras? Fortunately, we have still not reached the stage where the law obligates us to be under the constant watchful eye of the police. She was using unusual links? They were unusual only for those who were not up-to-date on innovations in the digital world. The police's cybernetics department should be more diligent about their job.

In fact, I was the only one who might gain anything from Ivana's arrest. Now everything I wanted and had the right to know would be clarified, and it was uncertain whether she would reveal it all to me herself. It most certainly was my business to know where the woman with whom I live had spent the night; how and why she was doing all that which had turned my world topsy-turvy in a mere half a day; who was collaborating with her in it.

When my cell phone suddenly rang, I—lost in thought—jerked upright as if something had popped on my desk.

"Ms. Mrvaljević…" I exclaimed.

"New problem. Ms. Đurić disappeared before we could get to her."

I was barely able to refrain from making a fist. At the last moment, I remembered she could see me.

"Disappeared?" I repeated, feigning confusion. "How did she disappear?"

"She slipped into a side street. All traces end there."

"You have no cameras there?"

"We do have one, but it's been blocked by a tall van they're unloading something from at the moment."

"Bad luck, that."

The inspector did not continue immediately. I could almost feel her sizing me up distrustfully. My tone of voice in that last sentence must have sounded suspicious to her, even though I had tried to sound truly sorry about their setback. However, she got past it.

"Does Ms. Đurić know anyone in Karaburma?"

"In Karaburma?" This time I did not have to pretend: I was truly surprised. "So, she was seen there?"

"Yes. Does she have any relatives or friends in that part of town? Acquaintances? Anyone she might be able to visit?"

"Since we got together, she has never been in Karaburma. Before that, I do not know. She has never mentioned anyone from there."

"How about you? Do you know anyone there?"

I had to think for a moment. "No. No one with whom I am in the least close."

"All right. It doesn't matter. We've surrounded the location where she is. We're sweeping the area from building to building. We're doing Ms. Đurić a great honor. We didn't use this much manpower even when we were capturing the biggest honchos in the underworld."

"You shouldn't compare Ivana to criminals. She has done nothing illegal. This is all one huge misunderstanding. You'll see as soon as you talk to her."

"That's what we're trying to do, but still can't. I hope we will soon." She stopped for a moment and changed the subject. "Did you maybe recognize the book Ms. Đurić put in the corners of the room?"

"I did not. The title was illegible."

"It remains illegible even under magnification. That's unusual because it's a high-resolution recording. I thought maybe you recognized the book by the cover."

Again I thought for a while. "No, I don't remember ever seeing it. Why is the title important?"

"It could be. You never know." She paused again. This time some sort of activity on the other end of the line could be heard. "I apologize, I have to hang up again. We have a situation…"

I was not well-informed about the jargon of the Belgrade police, but in films and TV series in English, the mention of a "situation" does not bode well. What exceptional thing could have happened now for a "situation" to come about? Nothing occurred to me other than that some sort of trouble had come up during Ivana's arrest. If she offered resistance, they would not hesitate at all to use force. Perhaps even weapons. I shuddered at the thought.

If someone had mentioned only yesterday that Ivana might be entangled with the police in any way, I would have just laughed. After everything that had happened the night before, however, there was nothing at all funny about the possibility that she might resist a legion of armed policemen on her trail.

The image of a large number of policemen pursuing Ivana conjured up another, less awful but just as disturbing. Such far-reaching police involvement could not remain a secret. The media had surely found out that something big was happening and rushed to the scene. From there, the tabloid papers would be the first to report. They would find nothing disagreeable about the suspect on the Internet, but they would make up for that lack of information with twisted imagination. I dared not even think of how they would sully her.

And not her alone, it occurred to me just then. As soon as they gleaned that Ivana and I were in a relationship, and that is no secret, they would shift the focus to me. Public figures are considerably more fit for a smear campaign than anonymous ones. The headlines danced before my eyes:

Živković's Chick Demolishes Karaburma!
Suicide Bomber Inspired by Famous Writer!
The Demons of Serbian Literature!

Instinctively I reached for my cell phone to turn it off. They would start swarming at me at any moment. But I remembered at the last instant that it would not be agreeable in the least for Inspector Mrvaljević to be denied telephone contact with me, so I left it on. I would only answer if her number showed up on caller ID.

Minutes passed, but no ringing disturbed the quiet of my study. When a sound finally was heard, it came from the computer speakers, not the cell phone. A gong announced the arrival of Ivana's eighth e-mail.

I could not expect the inspector, busy with their "situation", to call me when I could watch the new video, so I had to determine that for myself. The first video had been the longest up till then—a little more than two minutes. It would be enough, I supposed, if I was patient for three minutes before clicking on the blue "link".

It was doubly good news that there were no calls from the journalist vultures. Firstly, those calls themselves are truly tortuous, and secondly, their absence meant that the search for Ivana was proceeding without dramatic turnabouts. It seemed I was rash in my assumption that the "situation" was related to events in Karaburma. Ivana's case was certainly not the only one the police were dealing with today.

The seventh room was some sort of classroom. Three

rows of five double desks, a series of tall windows along one wall that looked out onto a schoolyard full of greenery on a sunny summer's day, a teacher's desk in front of a large blackboard. On the desk was a small vase containing two purple wildflowers, a wooden pen holder, a thin pointer, a large globe and a glass half-filled with water, covered by a linen napkin.

Ivana entered after a mere six seconds. She shrugged somehow ruefully, as if justifying herself for being a bit tardy to class, then hurried towards the last desk in the middle row. She sat down, placed her purse and umbrella on the seat next to her, put her hands in her lap and stared straight ahead. She remained motionless for fifteen seconds or so, as if carefully listening to the lesson. Then she quickly looked over her right shoulder into the camera in the upper corner of the room. A smile flashed across her face, then she immediately turned her attention forwards again.

Fifteen more seconds passed before she suddenly raised two fingers high, as if wishing to answer an inaudible question from the invisible teacher. She impatiently waved her fingers so as not to go unnoticed, and almost jumped from her desk when, seemingly, she was asked to approach the board.

She got there with just a few quick steps, picked up a large yellow sponge in one hand, chalk in the other, stepped back briefly, observed the empty dark surface—and began fervently writing. She got up on her tiptoes to reach the top of the board. Her movements were abrupt, sharp, indicating self-confidence, knowledge. The empty space quickly filled with a series of numbers and symbols—a mathematics far beyond what is taught in schools.

I stared in confusion at Ivana, who otherwise stumbles even through the four fundamental skills of math. This does not bother her at all; she is convinced that life can be perfectly pleasant even without an excessive knowledge of the world of numbers.

She had gotten halfway through the blackboard when something began to happen. At first, it seemed to me that a fire had broken out in the hallway outside the classroom. White smoke billowed in through the crack under the door. Ivana looked at it for an instant, then went on writing undisturbed. Then I noticed, by the way the white cloud was spreading through the classroom, that it was not ordinary smoke; it remained close to the floor, rising quite slowly, like the kind they use at the theater.

When the video ended at one minute and fifty-seven seconds, it had reached Ivana's knees.

19

My cell phone rang at the very moment the image froze on the screen.

"Is Ivana all right?" I asked without wasting an introduction.

The inspector hesitated briefly before answering, as if she were choosing her words carefully.

"Probably so."

"Probably? Did she get hurt during her arrest? Wounded?"

"There was no arrest."

"What was the 'situation' all about then?"

"The operation in Karaburma has been stopped."

"Why?"

From the speaker an audible sigh could be heard.

"Ms. Đurić is not there."

"What do you mean? Where is she then?"

"In Banovo Brdo."

In a moment of confusion, I first asked, "What is she doing there?" Luckily, I immediately realized what a silly question it was, so I rushed to ask a smarter one. "I meant to say, how did she get from Karaburma to Banovo Brdo so quickly? She could hardly have made it even by helicopter…"

"The more so since there have been no helicopters above Belgrade today."

"How do you know she is in Banovo Brdo?" This

was not the smartest of questions either. I could have guessed the answer.

"She was caught on one of our cameras there."

"Are you sure it was her you recorded?"

"We have really good facial recognition software. It has never let us down before."

"What would happen if Ivana had an identical twin sister?"

"But she doesn't. We checked. Unless you know something we don't."

"As far as I know, Ivana only has a younger brother. That could also be someone who looks very like her. Is your software so accurate that it can detect look-alikes?"

"I don't know. We've never had such a case. However, there's something more complicated going on here. An incidental look-alike would perhaps be possible, but not one dressed completely the same as Ms. Đurić."

At first, I did not know how to respond to this.

"Very well, then," I chimed in after a brief silence, "how do you explain Ivana's impossible appearance in Banovo Brdo?"

"Not quite impossible. Perhaps there really is a look-alike, but her appearance there was not coincidental. Ms. Đurić could have somehow found out about her and convinced her to participate in all of this."

"How would she convince her? Who would agree to toy with the police?"

"She might have presented the whole thing as a harmless prank. A love story, for example. Then it wouldn't take much convincing."

"All right, so be it. We have a look-alike in Banovo Brdo who does not have a clue about what she is involved in. Then why did you call off the search for Ivana in Karaburma?"

"Because it's probably the other way around: the look-alike is in Karaburma, while the original is in Banovo Brdo. If it were me toying with the police, that's exactly what I would do. First the look-alike would show up somewhere to lure the police into a useless search for her. And even if we found her, we would most likely not learn anything we don't know already. We would just look ridiculous."

"So are you headed for Banovo Brdo now?"

"No, we're not. We can't move that much manpower from one part of Belgrade to another as Ms. Đurić teases us. We also have other ways to foil her plans. It's her mistake for underestimating us."

I shook my head.

"This is all really... insane... impossible... Ivana is the last person in the world who would play games with the police. She would never have anything to do with you. She doesn't even jaywalk. She has no reason whatsoever to act like this, nor is it in her nature to do so..."

"I agree. Until last night, Ms. Đurić was a model citizen. But sometimes, things happen to such people... unexpectedly... out of the blue... As if they suddenly snap, as we say. They become the exact opposite of themselves. You can't recognize them. I've encountered such types. Fortunately, they're quite rare. Their common trait is that the reason for the sudden change is something simmering in their immediate surroundings, in the family. That's why I asked you if there had been any misunderstandings or arguments between the two of you..."

"I assure you there have not. I told you—we live harmoniously, no friction..."

"I'd like to hear what she has to say about that. She

invested enormous effort in making these videos. You don't do something like that without a very big reason. She's telling you something with them for sure. It's getting harder and harder to believe that you don't understand anything."

"I don't know how to convince you of it. I am completely in the dark. I neither recognize the rooms she is entering, nor do I understand the meaning of what she is doing in them. Not a thing."

"Not a single thing?"

I could almost feel her inquisitive look from somewhere behind me.

"Not a single thing," I repeated, unable to keep a soft tremor out of my voice.

"The classroom in the last video... you don't recognize it?"

"No. I no longer even remember the ones from when I was a pupil more than half a century ago, and they were different at college. This one I have certainly never seen."

"Ms. Đurić is really good at mathematics..."

"Better than I am, certainly. I did not understand anything she wrote down."

"And the white fog coming in under the door?"

"It looked like theatrical smoke to me."

"Interesting. I hadn't thought of that." Silence came from the speaker for a moment, as if she had covered the phone mike with her hand. "I apologize, I have to go."

"Another 'situation'?" I asked worriedly, but she had already hung up.

I turned off the video and stared at the e-mail window with Ivana's eight short messages. My vacant staring was interrupted by *force majeure*. I had to go to the bathroom.

Even though it was urgent, a sudden question stopped me at the bathroom door: had they put cameras in there as well? I tried to convince myself that they must have at least sufficient consideration not to watch me in the most intimate of places. What could I do there in secret anyway that would be of the least interest to them? True, I took my cell phone with me—not because I am an addict who goes nowhere without the device but because it was important I have it with me constantly on this remarkable day—but they could spy on my phone without having a camera in the bathroom. Still, I knew them well enough by now to realize that consideration was not one of their virtues. They would miss nothing out of mere thoughtfulness. And so, I went into the bathroom without turning on the light.

When I closed the door behind me, I found myself completely in the dark. Fortunately, I was well-versed in the actions for which I had come there, so I did not need the light. I remember that once I thought how, on a bet, I could complete the whole process blindfolded. Anyway, if I needed light, I could always briefly turn on the flashlight on my phone. I would not, of course, point the beam at myself, so they would not be able to record me half-naked.

I had already sat on the toilet when it suddenly occurred to me that they might have placed night-vision cameras in here. They had to suppose that I would do exactly what I had—that I would not turn on the lights. I became fidgety, but it was too late for me to change my mind. There was no going back. I lowered my head and covered my naked lap with my hands, even though nothing terrible could be seen even if there had been light. Unless the camera was in the toilet bowl itself, and I had not seen it when I checked after the forensics team had left. But they were not, hopefully, that perverted…

My real troubles began after I had finished. I knew, of course, where to reach out for the towel which would hide my nakedness as I stood up, but I had momentarily forgotten that my legs were hampered by the pants and underwear around my ankles. I tried to step forwards, but lost my balance. I misjudged the distance to the sink, so did not manage to grab it, but fell to the floor. It was not exactly painless, but what I found much worse was the thought that the police must be having a really good time watching a live broadcast of a famous writer's troubles in the pitch-black of his bathroom.

I lost my orientation and no longer knew where the towel was. I could search for it by feeling around, but I was no longer interested in entertaining the police voyeurs. I grabbed the first thing at hand—the floor mat I was sitting on—and wrapped it around my waist. Yet that was not the end of my troubles. To do what was necessary, I needed three hands, so it was inevitable that the toilet paper would roll away from me, that my plastic kilt would fall twice to the floor, that I would lose my left clog, that I would stub my toe on the washing machine, that I would hit my funny bone on the edge of the shower cabin. Finally, I emerged from the bathroom in tatters, flushed and messily dressed, as if I had just been a stand-in during the recording of a silent burlesque.

I was about to punch the button to call Inspector Mrvaljević and issue an angry protest against the police's maltreatment—not giving the slightest damn about their "situations"—when the sound of the gong rang out from my study. I rushed in, put my phone on the desk, unfastened my belt and spent a few minutes straightening my clothes, just enough time for them to watch the new video first. I did not care that I was doing this in front of others. After the bathroom, nothing was quite as embarrassing.

Ivana's ninth recording showed some sort of secondhand bookstore. It had high ceilings and, except for the cashier's desk, it was completely occupied by books. The walls could not be seen at all for the packed shelves. If the volumes on them were arranged in some kind of order, it was not obvious. Books of all formats, thicknesses, and colors were lined up in seemingly chaotic fashion, placed both upright and horizontally. An even greater disorder filled the floor. It was almost entirely covered with stacks of colorful volumes three feet high. There were narrow passageways alongside the shelves, and two intersecting ones which divided the great center island of books into an archipelago of four smaller ones. All of this seemed to be unstable, as if it might collapse at any moment. In the center of the bookstore, hanging on a long cord from the ceiling, was a bulb with a tin shade like a platter.

Ivana's entrance was announced by the tiny bells above the door. She stopped and spent a moment in curious observation, as if she were seeing the place for the first time. Glancing over the opposite wall, she waved at me with a smile when she saw the camera above the door that led into a side room. Then she headed towards the intersection of the paths that divided the island. She stood right under the bulb, took a book from one of the stacks, and focused on the blurb on the back cover.

She remained that way for twenty-odd seconds, then

she looked up startled, as if she had heard or felt something that was beyond my perception. She quickly returned the book, opened her umbrella, lifted it over her head and squatted down. Ultimately, all that could be seen of Ivana was the black dome of her umbrella resting its ribs on the top books of the center stacks.

Then it started.

A dull rumbling could be heard, and everything began to shake. The lamp and its shade rocked like a pendulum, making large arcs, and the stacks on the floor began to collapse and scatter. Quickly, the paths through the books and around the island disappeared. As the earthquake did not abate, the books first started to fall from above one by one, then three shelves pulled away from the upper part of the wall, tilting and casting their heavy contents all the way onto Ivana's umbrella in the middle of the bookstore. The video ended as hundreds of books completely covered the umbrella-dome. The chronometer stopped at one minute and thirty-two seconds.

How did they record this?—I wondered. Technically (it seemed to be quite convincing), but also in another sense. Ivana, in fact, was not particularly afraid of earthquakes—we had lived through one together, and I panicked more than she did—but she would never have agreed to be buried under a multitude of books, if only briefly and regardless of how protected she was. She feared nothing as much as being buried alive.

20

I CLOSED THE VIDEO window and called the inspector. Usually, she picked up right away; this time, the phone rang five times before she answered.

"How could you do that to me?" I got right to the point.

"What?"

"You had no right to put a camera in my bathroom. Night-vision at that. I could sue you for that. I demand that you immediately send someone over to remove it. It is completely unacceptable."

"We didn't put a camera in your bathroom," she answered with a flat, calm voice. "Neither a normal one nor one with night-vision."

"Do you expect me to believe you?" My voice had slightly lost its original ire.

"We are cooperating, Professor Živković. You remember? That means I tell you everything I can. I can tell you this. There is no reason for there to be a camera in your bathroom. You can be quite at ease there."

"How can I be at ease anywhere? When I just think that none of what has happened today would have occurred if only I had not called you this morning when Ivana's e-mail arrived. I did so in good faith, and where has it gotten me? I have cameras all over my apartment, you are watching my every move. To make no mention of the rest. And who knows what's next..."

"The fact that you informed us of the e-mail from Ms. Đurić is the best thing you've done. That's how we learned in good time about this extraordinary case, which is quite interesting for us. A case that's becoming more and more complex…"

I expected her to go on, but the inspector had fallen silent.

"A new 'situation'?" I broke the silence.

"Ms. Đurić and her look-alike were caught by two more cameras. This time, simultaneously. One of them was in Banjica, the other in Bežanija."

"How can that be? No one could get that quickly from one end of Belgrade to the other, even at break-neck speed."

"There has been no one going at breakneck speed. It's been an unusually quiet day so far. If we don't take this case into account, of course."

"Well, how then?"

"There is no simple explanation, I'm afraid. At the moment, we're investigating some more complex options. Even very complex. I still can't tell you about them. There is, however, something more important than 'how'. The main question is 'why'. If we answer that, 'how' will easily become clear. So, why is Ms. Đurić doing all this?"

She paused, expecting to hear what I had to say on the matter.

"All of it is still inconceivable to me. The Ivana I know does not behave like this. It would never even occur to her to toy with the police. Perhaps I do indeed not know her well enough, as you have suggested, but in the two years we have been together, she would have acted out some strange, eccentric side of her character at least once. She wouldn't be able to conceal it that long."

"Hmmm," responded the inspector.

"What's more, even if we assume that she managed to conceal her real face from me, she certainly couldn't have done all these other things by herself. Starting from the so-called links. By the way, have you learned anything about them?"

"Not yet. The 'links' are so unusual that even Interpol has gotten interested in them."

"How did they find out about them? Did you let them know?"

"No. They themselves discovered some sort of… disturbance… in the Internet connections here. They are also investigating now. The case has gone international."

I drew a deep breath. "And I was living so peacefully until last night…" Then a thought crossed my mind. "Is it possible that Ivana is a victim of some sort of… plot… from abroad? You know, a foreign service is using her to create a diversion here. That would explain a lot…"

"It can't be excluded. It's one of the possibilities we're looking into. And not just us, but also the military counterintelligence agency. Their expertise includes possible military operations abroad that could endanger our national security."

I had my hand over my mouth for several moments.

"Good Lord, how far has this gone…"

"Does Ms. Đurić have any foreign contacts? Does she write to people abroad, visit them?"

"Ivana has friends and business partners in various countries. She's been in contact with some of them for years. But they are all just ordinary people. I have even met some of them."

"Maybe it just seems that way…"

"Oh, really now. That is just paranoid."

I instantly regretted saying this. It might seem like an insult.

"Paranoia is a useful tool in my work, Professor Živković," she replied without a hint of offence. "Didn't you just ask if Ms. Đurić might be the victim of some sort of foreign service?"

"I did, although I see no reason why they would choose her of all people."

"Maybe because they can somehow compromise her into cooperating."

"How could they compromise Ivana into cooperating?"

"Mainly they use blackmail or bribery. They also use gullibility, the naïveté of those they're recruiting."

"They don't have anything to use on Ivana. They'd be able to bribe her even less. She is, actually, a little naïve, but not to the extent that she would allow foreigners to use her against her own country."

"There are other ways…"

"Whatever way they chose, what is the point of it all? Some foreign service stoops to a truly complicated plot just to play hide-and-seek with the Belgrade police?"

"Hide-and-seek is just the beginning. Who knows what else they're up to."

"I don't know what will happen next, but there's a more simple explanation for all this than its being the handiwork of a foreign service. Hackers."

"How would hackers convince Ms. Đurić to cooperate with them? She doesn't really move in those circles, does she?"

"They could have hidden the fact that they are hackers. If they introduced themselves, let's say, as students of film directing, I believe she would have agreed to appear in a series of their short films without double-checking, and later at their launch. She is just about that naïve. It would all seem fun and challenging to her."

"But wouldn't she tell you what she was getting into?"

"Maybe she wanted to surprise me."

"If they were hackers, they wouldn't be satisfied just to send the videos to you. They would attack the police system. But there has been no such attack."

"Not yet. But as you just said, who knows what's coming next."

The inspector was quiet for a moment. When she spoke out again, she seemed to lower her voice.

"Whoever is behind this—a foreign service, hackers, or someone else—why did they choose Ms. Đurić?"

I just squinted at the screen for a moment, then shrugged. I did not have the foggiest idea why they would choose Ivana.

"That's what this is all about, Professor Živković."

"What are you planning now?"

"I can't tell you about that. But we've gotten more manpower. We'll be more efficient than we have been up to now. By the way, did you maybe recognize the bookshop from the last video?"

I shook my head. "I did not."

"It's strange, but for a moment I thought I recognized it. I can't remember where from. Probably on the Internet. I like to visit libraries and bookstores online." Again there was a short pause. "We'll talk soon, professor. Go ahead and use the bathroom. You have my word that it's safe."

Getting up from my desk, I looked at the clock in the lower right-hand corner of the screen: 13:51. Was it that late already? Time passes quickly when the day is full of excitement. As if reacting to this information, my stomach growled. I usually eat around three, but today I had grown hungry earlier, probably also from the excitement.

As I entered the kitchen, I realized that for lunch I had only Ivana's uneaten supper from the night before and some salad. I had completely forgotten to go shopping. I could have used the opportunity while the forensics team was here, but in the direction Ms. Mrvaljević had sent me, there were, unfortunately, no shops.

If I had not been aware that they were watching me, I would not have set the table. As it was, I spread out a tablecloth, then took the salad from the refrigerator. It was not without a bad conscience that I again put the dish of food in the microwave. Ivana was sure to be hungry upon her return, and I would have nothing to offer her. Besides, I would also need something for supper. I would mention it to the inspector next time. She had told me not to leave the apartment again, but they would have to let someone bring me a delivery. They would not, I hoped, force me to go hungry.

Two sounds blended into one: a beep from the microwave informing me that my lunch was warmed, and a gong from the study, which most likely meant Ivana's tenth message had arrived. I only hesitated for a moment, then opened the microwave and took out the dish. Anyway, I had to wait for them to see the new video first, so there was actually no hurry. It made no difference if I saw one more of Ivana's cryptic messages a few minutes earlier or later. Like any wonder that repeats itself, her videos had stopped casting all else into the shadow. Hunger, for example, came to the fore.

Yet I did eat a little faster than usual, and I was not

as meticulous in washing the dishes. As I brushed my teeth in the bathroom, likewise hurriedly, I tried to convince myself that I could trust the inspector's promise. She had not deceived me so far. Here there were no cameras. Still, the skin crawled on the back of my neck as if I could feel someone watching me. The clock showed 14:14 when I returned to the computer.

Once again, there was an enclosed space—not a room, but a first-class compartment on a train. It was being recorded by a camera above the window, so there was no outside view. It seemed stylized and fancy, as if staged. Almost everything was dark red: the velvet used to upholster the three comfortable seats, almost armchairs, on each side, the rug as thick as a carpet, the heavy drapes gathered over the door. The chandelier hanging close to the high ceiling had five candle-shaped bulbs which shed a bright light.

Between the two seats by the window, a table had been pulled out, upon it a chessboard. The pieces were not in the starting position. Seven of them stood beside the board: four white, three black. As if someone had played a game, but I could not determine whether it had been finished or interrupted for some reason.

The roll of the door sliding open announced Ivana's arrival. She entered sideways between the gathered curtains. She did not push them aside, so the corridor could not be seen. She stopped briefly upon entry, looked around the compartment, smiled in satisfaction, waved at me, then set her purse and umbrella down on the first seat to the right. Her wide dark red woolen scarf was in perfect accord with the overall color-scheme of the compartment.

She approached the chessboard, briefly stood looking down over it, then sat in the left seat and coquettishly crossed her legs. She placed her left elbow on the table, rested her chin on her thumb and forefinger, and contemplated the setup. The camera began to zoom in on the board until it covered the entire screen. On the lower part of the monitor, a caption appeared: "Black moves and wins."

I have played chess since childhood, so I immediately understood why the task was difficult: there were too many pieces on the board, and they were all there for a reason. This problem could not be solved quickly. At least not by me. I moved closer to the screen and also contemplated the problem.

About half a minute passed, after which I was no wiser than at the start, when Ivana's arm in her overcoat suddenly entered the screen. With three fingers, she elegantly picked up the black pawn on H7 and moved it to H6. As she went out of shot, loud applause roared from the speakers for about ten seconds. It fell silent as the video ended at exactly one and a half minutes.

They must, of course, have trained Ivana on which move to make. Someone like her, who is not even sure how the pieces move, could not—especially not that quickly—have solved a problem meant, most likely, only for grandmasters.

21

I WENT ON STARING at the screen in front of me, asking myself if it was finally time for me to tell the inspector about these tiny oddities accompanying Ivana in the videos. In each of the ten recordings, there was something that was not characteristic of her. Something that only I could have noticed. What was the purpose of these deviations from the Ivana I knew? They were hardly accidental, precisely because they did not fail to appear every single time. What was the message they were meant to send me? I still could not even begin to fathom this, so it would be better not to say anything about them to Ms. Mrvaljević just yet. She would hardly believe that I had not discovered any meaning in them. And if she concluded that I was hiding something from her, she would start to deprive me of the cooperation which was so vital to me.

Submerged thus in thought, I gave a small jump when my phone rang.

"We have a new situation, Professor Živković," said the inspector. "Another look-alike has appeared."

At first, I did not know how to respond to this.

"How do you know it is a different one?" I finally inquired.

"We had all three of them on screen at the same time. One was in Rakovica, the second in Neimar, and the third in Senjak."

"Unbelievable. And?"

"And nothing. They remained within camera range just long enough for the software to recognize them."

"You didn't take any action?"

"There was no opportunity. By the time we reached any of those places, they would've been gone. We already know that they're quite skillful at disappearing quickly and covering their tracks."

"But that means, then, that you are powerless against them. That they can play hide-and-seek like this with you whenever they like."

"It's not smart to play hide-and-seek with the police…"

A brief silence ensued.

"All three were dressed the same?" I was the first to continue.

"Completely."

"Then how did you identify Ivana?"

"We didn't. That's the other reason we didn't take action when they appeared. Maybe we could have reached one of those places in a flash, but there was no certainty that Ms. Đurić would be in that particular place. As I already told you, it wouldn't be of much use to capture one of the look-alikes, so we just did nothing."

"But where could this new double have come from? The very possibility that one was found… that Ivana would find her… is minute. Two is completely impossible."

"Not completely. We're currently executing an extensive search: we're checking the photographs of all Ms. Đurić's contemporaries throughout the whole country. We're looking for those who are quite similar to her. There could be more of them than you would suppose. That way, we should be able to establish the identity of the two who have appeared so far, but also of others who might yet appear."

"But how could Ivana ever find them? She doesn't have the big databases at her disposal that you do. Fine, one look-alike she might have met accidentally, but not more than that."

"Remember, Professor Živković, that Ms. Đurić is not alone in this. You mentioned hackers last time. If she joined forces with them, then our databases might be available to her. There's no doubt that all of this was carefully planned long beforehand."

"But did you not tell me that there have been no recent hacker attacks on the police system?"

"I did. However, hackers are improving all the time. Maybe they managed to enter our system without leaving a trace. That possibility is also being considered now."

"Whatever the case, I refuse to believe that Ivana 'joined forces' with hackers against the police, as you just indicated."

"It doesn't seem that she's participating in this against her will. To the contrary, it's as if she's having a lot of fun playing games with us."

"Maybe it's all an illusion. Maybe she is being forced... blackmailed..."

"She's not being held in a dungeon. She's wandering freely around the city. Too freely, actually. If she were being forced or blackmailed, she could easily turn to us for help."

"Ivana is a serious woman, not a thoughtless juvenile. She would certainly be aware of the consequences of taking an irresponsible attitude towards the police. Though it might not seem so, I am convinced that she is someone's victim... that she is innocent..."

"And I'd be happy if it turns out that way in the end, but right now, it certainly doesn't look like it."

Again we fell briefly silent.

"I never would have guessed that Ms. Đurić plays chess," the inspector changed the subject.

"Why?"

"I don't know. She doesn't look like a chess player to me. Although, to be fair, I don't know what chess players should look like."

"Your impression was not incorrect. Ivana does not play chess at all. Someone told her which move to make."

"Do you play chess?"

"Do I look like a chess player to you?"

"More than Ms. Đurić."

"Thank you for the compliment. I used to play more often when I was younger."

"Then you've certainly heard of Nimzowitsch."

"Of course. The Nimzowitsch Defense. Why do you ask?"

"The final position in one of his games is on the video. Maybe you know about it?"

"I just saw it for the first time."

"The game was famous for its forced moves. The so-called *Zugzwang*. I thought they chose it because of that. As some sort of message…"

"Message—to whom?"

"To you. Her e-mails are arriving at your address, aren't they?"

"If it was meant for me, then they sent it in vain. If you hadn't told me, I would have had no idea whose game it was or why it was famous. It seemed to me that it was a chess problem. In any case, there are no forced moves related to me." I hesitated for a moment. "How about you? Do you play chess?"

"Do I look that way to you?"

"I don't know how you look. I do not have the privilege of following a live feed directly from your office..."

I expected her to react to this, but she changed the subject again.

"This compartment is also familiar to me from somewhere. I think I saw a similar set design in a play once, but I can't remember which one. Strange. I have an excellent memory..."

I had nothing comforting or enlightening to say to her, so this time, I changed the subject. "I have a request. I need to go shopping. My refrigerator is empty. I have nothing in for supper..."

"Have them deliver it. That's better."

She hung up before I had a chance to protest. Maybe it was better for them, but not for me. I wanted to go out again not just to go shopping, but also to get away from it all. I was growing fatigued with the alternating e-mails from Ivana and conversations with Ms. Mrvaljević. Even had I been significantly younger, I would not be taking this constant tension well. For hours, ever since I'd got up, I had not had a moment's break, and no end to these stressful events lay on the horizon. Who knew how many more videos would arrive, and what more would happen in various parts of the city.

Just as I began assembling my order on the application in my phone, a gong rang out. I checked the inbox, saw that Ivana's eleventh message had arrived, and then continued. The list also had eleven items in the end. I sent it off to the store, and clicked on the link which was not really one.

I immediately realized that I was observing a room in a cheap hotel. It looked impersonally cold, full of kitsch. The color of the overly tight bedcover on the king-sized bed did not match at all with the color of the wooden frame. On the long chest of drawers along the left wall stood a small TV set, a DVD player, and a canary yellow bowl of fruit, possibly wax. The scene in the unframed picture above the bed appeared borrowed from an old postcard: a rippling sea into which the sun was dipping as a small fishing boat returned to port. In one corner of the room were a small round table and two shabby armchairs in which hardly anyone would ever wish to sit. In the middle of the table rose a garish vase with a single wilted flower. Perhaps also artificial.

The door could be heard unlocking. Ivana entered, closed the door behind her, looked into the camera above the opposite wall, licked her lips, then put the key with its heavy fob on the chest of drawers. Next she almost threw her umbrella onto the bed, picked up the fruit bowl, and approached the table.

Then the unexpected began to happen. Even though repulsed by dusty old stuff, without a moment of hesitation she sat down on one of the armchairs, which creaked beneath her. She placed the bowl in her lap and rummaged briefly through her purse. Taking out what she was searching for, she placed her purse on the other chair. I recognized the item in her hand only when she began to open a pocket knife. Where did she get it from?—I wondered in bewilderment. What did she need that for? For the police, this would be a weapon. Now they would add this to their charge sheet as well, as if there were not already enough things on the list.

She stared into the bowl as if unsure what to choose first, then took a peach and skillfully quartered it. So, it was not wax fruit after all. What did she want to do with it? No, it could not be! The fruit was unwashed.

Goodness knows how long it had stood there. In disbelief I watched as Ivana—ever the excessive stickler
for cleanliness—placed piece after piece of dirty peach
into her mouth, while pleasure spread across her face.

After the peach, it was time for an apricot, then a
strawberry, a plum, and an apple. Watching Ivana finishing them off with gusto, I stopped worrying about
the fruit being unwashed. It occurred to me that it
was only apparently so, but that the fruit was actually
clean. It had been washed just before the recording.
Why would those behind these videos harm their main
actress?

The danger loomed elsewhere. She did not dare to eat
the strawberry. Not even the cleanest one. She is allergic to them. She would get a rash as soon as it touched
her mouth. She can't even stand the smell of them. For
that reason, I too have not eaten them at home since
we got together. Now, however, it seemed that they
did not bother her at all. Perplexed, I stared at radiant
Ivana, frozen on screen, at the bottom of which it said
that the recording had lasted two seconds longer than
a minute.

22

I THOUGHT THE INSPECTOR would call me, so I remained sitting at my desk. I closed all the windows
on the screen and stared for a time at the darkness of
the desktop. I could have entertained myself by surf-
ing the web, as I do at times of leisure, but at the moment I had no desire to do so. And it would also not be
appropriate. It would leave a bad impression on those
surveilling me. There I would be, having fun while the
entire police force and a series of other services were
frenetically trying to find Ivana.

The phone, however, did not ring, so I finally got
up because it would look suspicious to them if I went
on staring at an empty screen, even though that, actually, was what I would have preferred to do. That
would most likely relieve my gathering stress a bit. I
did not step away from the desk immediately. Only after standing up did I realize that I didn't know what
to do with myself. Yet, as I could not go on standing
there because that would also rouse suspicion—when
someone is constantly keeping an eye on you, you have
to be careful of each and every step—I headed for the
kitchen, just to be going somewhere. There I opened
the refrigerator and briefly pretended to be checking
something, then went to the living room.

I could have sat in one of the armchairs and tried
to read *The Seventh Function of Language*, and if it did

not go well, just carry on pretending. But what if I got sleepy in the process? That would indeed be awkward. Really, to fall asleep in the middle of such a day! They certainly wouldn't take my age into account as a mitigating circumstance.

Not knowing what else to do, I went to the right-hand window and looked outside. It was not even three o'clock, and it had already begun to darken because in the meantime it had grown fairly cloudy. No one could be seen, which was not unusual. The three windows of my living room look out onto a small park between my building and the next one over. It's much more lively in summer than in winter; there was no one out, especially on such a cold day as today. Just as I thought I could stand there for as long as I wanted—what is more innocent than looking out the window?—the sound of an arriving SMS rang out from the study.

Rushing in, I was hoping it could be a message from Ivana. It didn't matter that the police would see it. A few words from her would be enough, just to know that she was alive and safe. Everything else could be sorted out. Unfortunately, the SMS was from the inspector: *Get away from the window, please.*

Though it was not of the utmost importance, I wondered first why she had not called me to say so. Perhaps she thought I would object and didn't have time to argue with me. And I really would have rebelled. If they already wouldn't let me leave the apartment, why would they forbid me from looking through the window? Why, even prisoners have that privilege. Perhaps they had reason to believe that Ivana was somewhere nearby, and that we might communicate through it? I had already started walking back to the living room, when I was stopped by a sudden thought. What if my own safety was at risk? Perhaps someone could harm me as I stood by the window. Ms. Mrvaljević had mentioned foreign services. I myself was certainly not of interest, but they could blackmail Ivana by using me. If you do not do this and that, the professor is a dead man. Maybe it would be best to close the shutters...

I shook my head. Why, that is just silly...

Just as I thought this, from the hallway, like a gunshot, the doorbell rang, making me flinch. Who was that now? The police? The inspector surely would have announced a visit. Ivana? Why would she ring the bell when she has a key? A foreign agency? I froze...

I would pretend not to be home. Yes, but they know that I am. They just saw me standing at the window. The inspector had warned me too late. Strange that they should ring instead of just busting in. No matter, they would do it at any moment when they saw that I was not opening up. Our door lock certainly wouldn't hinder them. What was I to do? I couldn't jump from the fifth floor. Where could I hide? I began to panic. No hiding place came to mind. Why were the police not intervening? They certainly had people nearby in case Ivana got here clandestinely. I did not have to warn them, they had heard the doorbell. What were they waiting for? I strained my ears, hoping to hear a scuffle in the hallway outside my door, a sign that the police were taking on the foreign agency, but everything was quiet.

Several long minutes passed before I mustered the courage to move. On my tiptoes, I approached the front door and had already leaned towards the peephole, when it occurred to me that they were waiting precisely for that. I had seen what they do in some movie about the mafia. They fire a shot through the peephole right into your eye. I stepped as close to the side as I could, slipped off my left clog, and put it in front of the peephole. No damage done if they shoot through it. The worst that could happen is that they wound my hand.

However, the expected gunshot never came. All remained quiet. Again, several minutes dragged on before I gathered the courage to peer out the peephole. The hallway was lit, but there was no one there. That still meant nothing. If they stood close to the wall next to the door, I would see nothing. The police, however, would see them. They must have put at least one camera in the hallway, just in case. Certainly they would have warned me if I was in peril.

With renewed hesitation, I took the key from the shoe cabinet. I unlocked the door almost silently, opened it a little, then quickly closed it. Since nothing happened, I opened it just enough to cast a look down the hallway in one direction. No one. Then in the other direction. No one. It was only when I looked in the third direction— just in front of me—that the enigma was solved.

I opened the door wide. In the bathroom perhaps there really were no cameras, so no one had seen my débâcle in there. Here, however, not only was everything seen, but also recorded.

On the doormat, there were two bags that had been delivered from the store. Whoever had brought them had waited for me to open up, then left after concluding that I was, perhaps, in the bathroom. He or she had certainly informed the doorman at the exit.

I took the bags, closed and locked the door, and returned the key to the shoe cabinet. No one asked me anything, so I did not have to explain. Pretending that this was all normal—that I always react with such precaution when someone rings the doorbell—I headed to the kitchen. I opened the refrigerator and started putting away the delivered food.

As I pulled out the last item, from the bottom of the bag I also retrieved the receipt which fluttered to the floor. I picked it up and was about to throw it in the garbage can, when I noticed that, through the thin paper, something could be seen written in marker on the back. I turned it over, and froze.

There was not a single letter. Just a banal mathematical equation: $11 + 11 = 22$. And beneath it, a small heart had been drawn. My own large heart began to pound. From the start of our relationship, Ivana had always signed her SMS texts with this emoticon.

I did not digress into deciphering the message immediately. That could wait. It was far more important not to allow those watching me to notice that something unusual had happened. I went on staring at the receipt, as if checking it, then went over to the garbage can and threw it away. There. Now they would suspect nothing, and I could retrieve it unnoticed the next time I threw something away. And even if I did not, I had memorized the simple message.

Just as I closed the lid, a gong rang out from my study. In my excitement, I headed there too quickly, which might have aroused suspicion in my observers at the police station. I slowed down. I was not in a hurry. About three minutes would pass before it was my turn to look at the twelfth video. I sat down at my desk, pretending to be idle as I waited, and gave myself over to my feverish thoughts.

Ivana could have written this only at the store or as the delivery person was on the way here. The latter would be simpler. I did not know if the store had its own deliverers, or if they hired one of the delivery services, but that was actually inconsequential. Whoever brought me the groceries, it was unlikely they would refuse a healthy tip just to allow someone to write a short message to the customer on the receipt. A love note, obviously, judging from the signature.

I left aside the much more difficult question: how did Ivana even know that I had ordered something from the store? No answer came to mind, but on this day full of surprises, this could probably also be explained somehow.

Then I was stricken by a thought. If they were watching me closely, I hoped they could not see by my face the turbulence in my soul. Perhaps no tip at all had been necessary. What if Ivana herself, disguised as a delivery person, had brought me the bags from the grocery store? (I had no idea how she could pull that off.) She would have thus cleverly deceived the police who were certainly checking everything and everybody at the building entrance.

You idiot!—I harshly reprimanded myself. Who knows how much effort she had invested to reach our front door, and you chose that moment to become fearful of some sort of foreign agency. And if she also saw how heroically you put your clog over the peephole instead of opening the door wide...

A new thought damped down my remorse. Ivana had not performed that whole performance just to see me for a second, but to deliver the message to me. That was important, not my latest disgrace. What did she want to tell me with those numbers?

There was no chance for me, however, to reflect on that because a new message arrived from the inspector with the same old command: *Watch*.

At first, I thought it showed a café. No one was sitting at any of the six small round tables with three chairs each. Almost all the surfaces were in some shade of purple: the wallpaper, rugs, tablecloths, upholstery, menu covers. So were the shades on the lighted table lamps. In the dim lighting, it was as if the air itself was hued in purple.

Then from the contents of the showcase by the counter I realized I was wrong. Such a selection of pastries could only exist in a pastry shop.

About ten seconds from the start of the twelfth video, Ivana came in as if skating into the frame, recorded from a camera above the front door. She stopped briefly, as if she needed a second for her eyes to adjust to the purple dusk. Then she went over to the nearest table, put her purse on one of the chairs, hung her umbrella on the back of the other, and sat down on the third.

She picked up a menu and began to peruse it. Her smile never left her face. The names of the delicacies must have been humorous. Finally, she tapped her right index finger twice on the middle of a page, as if she had chosen whatever was there, then closed the menu and put it on the table before her.

She raised her head and stared towards the counter, as if waiting for someone to come over and serve her. Since no one did, even after twenty seconds or so, she lost patience. She stood up, walked over the counter, then went behind it. From somewhere underneath it she pulled out a small plate and some silverware wrapped in a purple napkin. She opened the showcase from the back, looked around it, and having found what she was looking for, took the cake with a knife and fork and placed it on the plate.

She was just about to close the showcase when she

changed her mind. She put the filled plate on the counter and took another clean one. Soon, a second full plate appeared next to the first. She came out from behind the counter, picked up the two full plates, and went back to the table.

Even though it was clear what was about to happen, I stared in disbelief at Ivana as she began to dig in. Nothing like her usual self, with a teaspoon she began to scoop up large pieces of the rich purple cake and eagerly stuff them into her mouth. Her cheeks were constantly puffed out. The first plate was quickly cleared, and when she started in on the second without stopping, I shuddered, even though I knew that this could certainly not be real. Those could not be real pastries. As a diabetic, Ivana did not dare even lick anything sweet, far less gobble down two large pieces of cake like this.

The entire sugary insanity lasted just a minute and thirty-nine seconds.

23

THE INSPECTOR CALLED ME as soon as the recording ended.

"Ms. Đurić has a real sweet tooth."

"Only when the role demands. Otherwise, she is much more moderate. And she does not really enjoy sweets."

"Interesting. It wouldn't hurt if she were a little more moderate with us as well. Now there are five of them."

"What do you mean—five?"

"In the Fibonacci sense. First there was one, then she was joined by another. Then came the third, and now there are five. One, two, three, five. If it goes on like this, next time there will be eight, then thirteen… The progression is growing quickly. You know the sequence, right?"

"Of course I do. But that is not possible. Where would all the look-alikes come from?"

"We have no idea. In the whole country, we found only two women who could more or less pass as doubles for Ms. Đurić. Our facial software would not be deceived, though. It would differentiate between them. In addition, both of them live outside of Belgrade and are at home right now."

"Well, how then?" A thought flashed through my mind. "Or did they perhaps…?" I waved my hand in dismissal. "No, that is not possible…"

"What?"

"I thought that whoever involved Ivana in all this found her look-alikes abroad and then brought them here. The selection would be much greater there. But who would stoop to something like that just to play around with the police?"

"Maybe it's not playing around at all, but something much more sinister. Anyway, we checked the appearances of all foreigners who have entered Serbia in the last three months and are roughly the same age as Ms. Đurić. Not a single one of them resembles her even vaguely."

"So, what will you do now?"

"The only thing we can at the moment. We'll place all available personnel near to spots where there are cameras. Maybe we won't cover every single location, but we think this will be enough…"

"How many cameras do you have," I interrupted her, "when you don't have sufficient people to cover all of them?"

"Not enough yet. There will be enough only when there are no more blind spots." She said this as if she had missed the meaning of my question. Or, more likely, that she had overlooked it on purpose.

"Just awful," I mumbled to myself.

She went on, ignoring what I had said, "Then we'll wait for them to show up. The more there are next time, the greater the chances that we'll catch at least one. We're not choosy anymore. We're not looking just for Ms. Đurić. Her doubles will also be useful to us. We now believe that they must know a lot more than we thought at first. We'll do our best to get as much out of them as possible. If Fortune smiles on us, one of the look-alikes could be the original—Ms. Đurić herself."

"How will you know it is her? Shall you do your best to make each one confess that she is Ivana?"

"That will be unnecessary, and you misunderstood what I was saying. If the police were still like that, do you think I would be working here?"

I shrugged. "How could I know that? I do not know you."

"If you did, you would know that I'm much more similar to Inspector Dejan Lukić than some police bully."

I was tempted to respond that Inspector Lukić was feasible only in literature, but I restrained myself. As a reader of mine, the inspector deserved my civility.

"We have the DNA of Ms. Đurić," she went on, since I did not speak. "We gathered it at your place. That is much more reliable than any sort of forced confession."

"I would like to ask you something," I changed the subject. "Why did you tell me to move away from the window?"

"It's better that way. You can look out, of course, but please don't stay at the window for too long."

It was not worth insisting. In this sense, I was already quite familiar with her. She would tell me nothing more than 'it was better that way'.

"One other thing. Who delivered my groceries?"

Now I was expecting her to be discreet—by not mentioning my infamous opening of the door...

"A girl from the store. Why?"

Most fortunately, the inspector could not also observe how fast my heart was beating.

"I didn't get the credit card receipt," I responded, trying to keep the excitement from my voice. "Just the cash register receipt. Never mind, I will take care of it tomorrow when I go there."

The inspector was silent for several moments, as if considering my words. Then she changed the subject as well.

"The pastry shop from the last video..." she began, then stopped.

"Yes?"

"It's like a replica of one near the Church of St. Mark."

"Why a replica? Maybe they actually recorded it there."

"Impossible. It's been gone for years. There's a cosmetics store in that spot now. I used to drop by there occasionally. They had great puff pastries. I remember well that the place was all done in purple, just like in the video."

"I don't remember it at all. It's no wonder. I don't frequent pastry shops. The last time I patronized one I was still a college student."

"Interesting..." She must have muted her telephone at that instant because my speaker went silent. "I'm sorry, Professor Živković," she quickly came back on. "Duty calls. We'll be in touch."

As I set the telephone down on the desk, I had a sudden urge to drink coffee. I do not usually drink it after lunch, only in the morning, but caught up in the whirlwind of this wild day, I had completely forgotten about it. Here was a chance to compensate for that missed opportunity before a new video or new situation interrupted the lull. I got up, picked up my phone and went into the kitchen.

There is only one window there, so even in the summer, there is less light than in the other rooms. I raised my hand to turn on the light, but changed my mind. If I was really in danger from someone outside, as one might surmise by the inspector's vague warning not to stand in the window, I would be a still easier target if lit, even further away from the window. In addition, the dark interferes with cameras, and there was no reason to put night-vision ones in here. If they asked me to, I would, of course, turn the light on, but until then, I did not have to play into their hands.

It was not difficult to make coffee in the capsule machine even in the dim light. It seemed to me that I could do it with my eyes shut, so many times had I repeated the simple movements. When the apparatus began to growl and pour the hot brown beverage into my cup, I thought that the sound of the computer gong reached my ears, but I was not sure. Whatever the case, I restrained myself from immediately rushing to the study to check. If it was Ivana's thirteenth mail, I had just enough time to finish making coffee and clean the machine.

When I raised the garbage can lid to throw away the used capsule, I saw the receipt laying on top of the trash. I would not have seen it in the dim lighting if it were not white. I did not shake the capsule holder empty from high up, but lowered it into the can. As the capsule slipped out, I snatched the receipt up with two fingers and raised it with the holder. They could not have noticed this, even if the camera was just above my head. I returned the holder into the machine together with the receipt. Voilà! They would never think to look for it there.

I took the cup and headed to the study. My patience was weak, so along the way, I took a hot sip. It started working immediately. As if something refreshing was spreading through my stomach. So, the provisions had been brought by some girl. Could they have disguised

Ivana to look thirty-odd years younger? In any simpler situation, I would have concluded that it was impossible, although I would never have offered that opinion out loud in her presence. Today, however, I was not so sure, keeping in mind that the numerous look-alikes were so well-disguised as Ivana that the facial recognition software had succumbed to trickery.

If it was not Ivana after all, but really just a girl, then everything had been done in the store itself. The simplest explanation was that they had somehow convinced a cashier to write a short message to me discreetly on the back of the receipt. The inspector had no reason to be watching her. Perhaps I should not have mentioned the credit card receipt. That might lead her to watch the surveillance footage from the store. Still, if they came to look for the receipt, they would not find it in the garbage can.

Why, however, was it necessary to involve a cashier just to send me a message I did not understand? (Leaving aside for a moment the question of how they found out that I had ordered something from the store.) Indeed, what more profound meaning other than the obvious could be held in $11 + 11 = 22$? Just the two elevens crossed my mind: the message had arrived after the eleventh video, and my shopping list contained eleven items. I saw no connection between the two. What would there be twenty-two of if these elevens were added?

Anyway, this was not the time to delve into the puzzle. With a new SMS, Ms. Mrvaljević gave me the green light to watch Ivana's thirteenth video. I sat at the monitor, took two more sips of coffee, put the cup and my phone on the desk, and clicked on the "link".

There was a small circular space with white walls. It

was brightly lit by three bulbs hanging on long cords from the high ceiling. Although whatever was moving them could not be seen, they oscillated rhythmically like the apexes of an equilateral triangle. In the middle of the little room stood a circular table. It had only one thick leg, fastened to the floor. Behind the table rose a large barrel.

The movement of the light-shedding pendulums quickened when Ivana entered the room. She approached the table, set down her purse and umbrella on it, and went around the right-hand side of the barrel. There must have been some small steps, probably wooden, invisible to the camera above the door. Climbing them, Ivana rose in her entirety above the barrel. As if she were about to execute a circus act, she bowed deeply, waved at me with both hands, and stepped into the barrel with a smile. There were obviously some wooden steps inside as well. She descended by them and completely disappeared into the barrel.

Nothing happened for at least half a minute. Even the undulations of the light bulbs stopped. Ivana's next appearance was announced first by a thundering fanfare. Simultaneously, the light bulbs came back to life, but now with no rhythm. They danced wildly about, miraculously avoiding colliding with one another.

I squinted to look at Ivana's hair. She was wearing a bright red wig, woven into a braid as thick as an arm. It was tossed forwards. When she mounted the first step, the edge of the barrel was just beneath her chin. Nothing could be suspected at that moment. However, as soon as she mounted the second, everything became clear. Other than the wig, she was not wearing anything. Her shapely breasts glowed, separated by the braid whose tip had not yet appeared.

I had not even managed to be surprised, and Ivana was already on the third step. She had emerged to just beneath her waist, and the braid was still going on. Surely she will not climb to the fourth? I wondered in bewilderment.

She did not. Or rather, perhaps she did, but the video stopped there. At the fifty-seventh second. I quickly closed the window, as if I could thus somehow stop something from happening. Many other eyes had already seen the recording.

24

I FINISHED MY COFFEE and took the cup to the kitchen. As I washed it in the sink, still leaving the light off, my phone rang. Why is she calling me now when even in the dim light they can certainly see that my hands are wet? I raised them into the air to show her what should have been obvious to her, but then it crossed my mind that it was perhaps not the inspector.

I had thought it was her mostly because I had only talked to her today. Only now did it occur to me that no one else had called, and here it was, almost four in the afternoon. I could not remember a day when everyone had forgotten me like this. On the contrary, I was usually complaining because people interrupted my work for insignificant reasons. Ivana had soberly suggested that I turn off my phone while working, as she did, but I continued to leave it on so that I would not miss an important call. Such calls almost never happened, but the disturbances did. In abundance. Until today.

I perfunctorily dried my hands on the dishtowel hung over the sink, then hurried to the study before my phone stopped ringing. It was the inspector after all.

"I'm sorry for not answering immediately," I said in a reproachful tone. "You saw the reason."

Ms. Mrvaljević paid no heed to my words. "Did you notice the moles on Ms. Đurić?"

"The moles?"

"Yes. Two on her left breast and one on the right. They are small. You wouldn't have seen them if the camera weren't high-resolution."

I reflected for a moment. "No, I was not paying attention to that. Why?"

"But you know that she has them, right?"

Again I was slow to answer. "Now that you mention them, I vaguely remember some moles, but if you hadn't told me, I wouldn't be sure that she had them, and even less so how many on which breast. I would really have to strain to remember..."

"Ah, male memory..." sighed the inspector.

"All right. I will heap ashes upon myself. Just as I do not have an eye for female wardrobe, I also do not have one for female moles. Moreover, I do not count them when they are in front of my eyes because my attention is then elsewhere. Why are the moles even important?"

"We want to make sure that Ms. Đurić really disrobed herself."

"Of course it was Ivana. You don't need moles to recognize her. You saw her head."

"The look-alikes have the same head. Our software does not differentiate them."

This caught me off guard. How was it that such a possibility never crossed my mind?

"I am better than your software," I tried to get myself out of trouble. "I most certainly recognize the woman I love."

"What feature makes you so certain it was her?"

"Everything... Her overall posture... the way she walks... her facial expressions... gestures..."

"But not also her moles. And that would be the only feature that positively differentiated her from her look-alikes. All the rest can be copied."

"And moles could be drawn on."

"They could be, if it was known that she even has them. But that is not generally known, right?"

"All right, I didn't memorize her moles, but I do know the shape of her breasts, nipples… It is Ivana, trust me."

"You can't judge by that. The number of shapes is really small; women have quite similar breasts to other women. As far as nipples go, you just said yourself that your attention is elsewhere, so you don't notice details when they're right in front of your eyes. But let's forget about that now. There's something more important. Would Ms. Đurić ever agree to disrobe in public?"

For several moments I just looked at the screen, wordless. Finally, I shook my head. "She would not. Unless she was being blackmailed or forced."

"Why would they do that, when there's a much simpler solution? Instead of her, one of her doubles could have performed."

I didn't know how to respond to this, especially because there was a lot of sense in the idea. The inspector waited a moment, then broke into the silence by changing the subject. "Unusual ambience in the thirteenth video…"

"Echoes of Magritte…"

"My thoughts exactly. As if it were taken directly from one of his paintings. I'll have to…" She did not finish her sentence. "I'm sorry…" This time the microphone remained on, but I did not manage to discern what the muffled voices were saying. Several seconds later, the inspector just said succinctly, "Look-alikes!" and hung up.

I put my phone on the desk and sat down. Ms. Mrvaljević's idea that it was not Ivana in the thirteenth video but a double was more profound than she imagined. What—I wondered—if it was a look-alike in the preceding twelve recordings as well? That would explain many of the peculiarities about Ivana that I had noticed in each video, but had not mentioned to the inspector…

For this postulation to be accepted, however, at least three questions had to be answered. First was the old one: where were all the doubles coming from? Then, in the videos, was only one of them appearing or more of them? For the moment, we knew there were four or five, but the inspector was expecting more, so there could be a different one in each recording. Finally, why would look-alikes replace Ivana at all? In the disrobing episode, all right, but there was nothing immoral in the other twelve.

I sat a while longer reflecting on these conundrums, but did not manage to resolve a single one. Tough questions without answers had rained down on me since the night before, and instead of something illuminating, everything was just becoming more opaque. The darkness in the apartment was growing deeper, as if it were a metaphor of what was inside me. And while the latter apparently could not be resolved, it was easy to change the former.

I turned on the light on the desk, then got up and started turning them on all over the apartment. I went from room to room, pressing switches until everything was eventually bathed in light. At our place, the lights in the evening are otherwise subdued, so from the outside one might now think we were having a celebration. I did not much care if this would make it significantly easier for the cameras, or if the police would conclude that I was maybe sending secret signals this way to Ivana. The only important thing to me was to inject a little light into my life.

Out of breath from walking quickly through the apartment, I returned to the study right at the instant when the gong signified the arrival of Ivana's four-teenth e-mail. For the first time, I was grateful that I had to wait for the police to watch it first. I needed a short break. I sat at the desk, expecting Ms. Mrvaljević to send me an SMS approval. Since it did not arrive even after four minutes, I clicked on the "link".

It took several moments before I realized that the stage for the new video was a windowless exhibition hall in a gallery or museum. I was confused by the shapes of the thin frames. Their sizes differed, but every last one was triangular. The pictures they framed were mostly of a bright, even glaring color scheme, in harsh contrast with the pale yellow walls. A spotlight from the ceiling was trained on each canvas. In the center of the room was a wide bench upholstered in leather.

After about ten seconds, Ivana stepped through the doorless entryway, obviously from a neighboring hall. She approached the bench and set her purse and umbrella on it, then started looking at the paintings. They were all hung at head height. She would stop briefly at each, sometimes drawing closer, sometimes standing back a little. They were works of abstract art.

Having looked at all the canvases on one wall, she moved to the next. That particular one was opposite the camera so I could not see immediately what was in the first painting because Ivana was blocking it. She shook her head two or three times, went over to the bench, and looking left and right as if making sure no one was watching, she opened her purse, pulled something out, then turned and went back to the picture.

I saw what she had taken out and what was painted

when she stepped back to wave a large pair of scissors towards the figurative canvas she had come across—a triangular male portrait. Her movement remained incomplete because the recording stopped at one minute and forty-three seconds.

This had to be a look-alike, I concluded adamantly. Ivana would never, ever destroy an artistic work, no matter how much she disliked it. Much less a piece where I was the subject of the painting...

༄ 25 ༀ

I EXPECTED THE INSPECTOR would call me as soon as the video finished, but the minutes passed and the phone before me on my desk did not make a sound. It must be that something significant was going on with the look-alikes she had mentioned at the end of our last conversation. I had no idea what that could have been. She expected the number to continue to grow in a Fibonacci sequence, but that was unthinkable. It was already hugely unbelievable that even one double had appeared that could deceive the police's facial recognition software; everything beyond that was simply inexplicable.

The inexplicable had become quite common with almost everything that had happened in relation to Ivana's disappearance since last night. Her impossible "links", the mysterious videos, the camera avoidance, her lightning fast movement across the city (if that had even happened), the enigmatic message on the back of the grocery store receipt, and above all, the lack of any sort of sense in what she was doing. To be fair, perhaps there was some sense, but neither I nor the police were capable of grasping it. She might have her reasons for keeping the police in the dark, but why me? Why had she not at least given me a hint about what she was up to? Perhaps I could have been of some use to her.

I jerked back noticeably when the phone rang. Convinced that it was the inspector, I quickly put it to my ear without looking to see the caller ID.

"What is the news?" I asked impatiently.

There was no answer.

"Hello?"

I waited a bit longer, but instead of the inspector finally saying something, the connection was severed. In confusion, I pulled the phone away and looked at the screen. On it, there was not a trace of a phone call. I looked at the list of received calls—the long series of the inspector's calls, the last of which had been twenty-odd minutes before. How was that possible? I was certain I had not imagined the phone ringing. If nothing else, the green circle had appeared to make the connection. I had swiped my index finger across it. Even if nothing could be heard on the other end, the call must have remained recorded nonetheless.

I jerked back again when the phone rang anew, but this time, I held it up and looked at the screen. Now it could be seen who was calling.

"Turn on the speakerphone, please," said Ms. Mrvaljević.

I did so.

"Now, put the phone on the desk."

Again I obeyed. Before my very eyes, the pictures on the screen began to change, even though my hands were in my lap. It took me several moments to figure out that the police had remote access to my phone and were in the process of doing what I had just done—checking to see if some trace of the previous call remained.

"Do you know from whom the call came?" I asked when the screen went blank.

"We don't, though we should. Judging by all things, Ms. Đurić continues to have fun at our expense…"

"You have no proof that it was her…"

"We don't, but since no one else could have called without leaving a trace, the suspicion immediately falls on her."

"Why would Ivana call me, and then not say anything?"

"There, just one more question which only she can answer. Perhaps she is having fun at your expense too, who knows? Anyway, that's a small problem in relation to the ever bigger one with the look-alikes."

"What is happening on that front? How many of them have appeared?"

"Eight."

"Impossible! Ivana does not have that many doubles in the whole world."

"At the moment, we're troubled by something else—the places where they appeared."

"The places?"

"Yes. We had people in proximity to almost all the cameras. There were only eight unattended in out-of-the-way places…"

"You wish to say…"

"The doubles were seen in precisely those places."

"That certainly cannot be a coincidence…"

"Clearly not."

"Well, how then?"

"Simple. They somehow found out which places were not under surveillance."

"What do you mean—'somehow'?"

"Either someone with access to the police systems alerted them…"

"Someone in the police?"

"For example. We already mentioned that. We checked out that possibility, but we didn't discover anything. Now we're checking again. More thoroughly."

"Or...?"

"Or whoever is behind all this got into the police systems by themselves. Unnoticed. That is also being checked again right now. Even more thoroughly than the first."

"What would have happened if there were more unattended places? Would there have been the same number of look-alikes?"

"We can only guess. In any case, if the doubles appear again, next time, we'll be completely prepared. We asked for more manpower and got it. From outside the capital. We'll have someone near every camera."

I did not know how to respond to this, so we were silent for a moment.

"Now, about the fourteenth video..." the inspector spoke up first. "I had no idea that triangular picture frames exist until I read about it in one of your books."

"Which one?"

"Don't you know?"

"I can't remember."

"How unusual. I always thought that writers remember perfectly everything they've written."

"They do until they reach the age when they start forgetting what really happened as well as what they made up."

"That's really sad."

"No, not really. I would actually like to forget everything I've written."

"Why?"

"Then I could read my own books again. Like Knut Hamsun. The Norwegian…"

"I know who Knut Hamsun was."

"You see, Hamsun suffered from Alzheimer's. He forgot that he had ever been a writer. Then they gave him his own books to read again. He was delighted. He said that their young author was bound to be famous one day…"

"Sad…"

"Of all the infirmities that can overcome you in old age, senility is actually the most desirable. There is no pain at all, and every day you learn something new… So, in which of my books…"

"Excuse me," she broke in suddenly, and then hung up.

I closed the video window and opened the folder where I keep saved all my prose texts. In it, there is also a file in which all my books are laid out chronologically. I use it to facilitate searches when I want to establish something that is related to my entire body of work. I searched "triangular frames". Not because I did not know in which book I had mentioned them—of course, I knew; the moment had not yet come for me to read my own books again as if for the first time. I wanted to check something that perhaps five years before I would not have had to, but at the age of seventy-three I did.

I sat looking for a long while at a paragraph in the fourth chapter of *Miss Tamara, the Reader*, unaware of the passing of time. I would most gladly have somehow chased away the thoughts swarming through my mind, but they were firmly ensconced and did not wish to depart. They were driven out only by the sound of the gong announcing the arrival of Ivana's fifteenth e-mail.

I closed the text processor, went to the kitchen and poured a glass of water, even though I was not thirsty. I had to occupy myself until I got permission to look at the new recording, and nothing else came to mind. I drank the water slowly, as if it were some expensive drink one swishes around in the mouth before swallowing it. I was taking the last swallow when the notification of the inspector's SMS rang out from the study.

It did not take me long to see that it was some sort of antique shop. It was poorly lighted and seemed untended. The walls of the small space were lined with dusty shelves holding a variety of old things, while in the center was an open showcase full of scattered small objects: a monocle without a lens, a snuff-box, a chipped medal, a marble ink blotter, a gilded tie pin, an ivory cigarette holder…

When Ivana entered, a bird's chirping could be heard from somewhere. She stopped at the door, right under the camera, as if expecting a salesperson to appear when a customer came in, but no one did. She stood in the doorway a while longer, glancing around the shop, then headed for the showcase. For the first time, she kept her purse and umbrella in the crook of her elbow.

She began looking with interest at the exhibited trinkets. She did so at a leisurely pace, as if making sure not to overlook anything. She bent over and from somewhere picked up a bundle of old letters, postcards, and fading photographs, tied up with a blue ribbon. She straightened up, blew the dust off the bundle, looked at it a bit more, then put it in her purse. From an oval tray on top of the showcase, she picked up a creamer from a tea service. She pulled out a teaspoon with a crest, looked up at the camera, smiled at me, and tossed it into the creamer. It resounded like a call bell.

She added these two objects to the bundle of letters, then went behind the counter on the left side. There, she rummaged around in her purse until she found her wallet. She pulled a bill from it, then pushed a key on the large antique cash register. The cash-drawer popped out of the register with a sharp sound. She put the bill into it, and closed the drawer with a decisive shove.

She dusted off her hands a little, then headed for the door. Along the way, she raised her free hand and, without looking at the camera, flapped her gathered fingers as if telling me "bye-bye". The recording stopped at two minutes and eleven seconds, at the moment when the door closed behind Ivana.

This was the first, and probably last, time that I had ever seen her in an antique shop. She abhorred such places. She simply could not understand people who were excited by antiques. For this reason, I now rarely visited these emporia of the past, even though I loved being in them.

⌒ 26 ⌒

I CLOSED THE VIDEO window, and again started moving the cursor towards the folder holding the file with my books in it. However, I did not open it. The hair on the back of my neck reminded me that I was being watched, that curious eyes were observing what I did on my computer, so I stopped. They did not have to see every step I made. Anyway, there was no need for me to open the file. I still knew what was written there...

I picked up my phone, got up, and went into the bathroom. I stared at the reflection of my face in the mirror above the sink. I remained like that for a moment or two, put the lid down on the toilet, and sat on it. I wanted to believe the inspector that there were no cameras here. I had a sudden urge to escape the surveillance for at least a moment. Now I was personally experiencing something that I had only read about earlier—when you know that you are being watched, it does not take long before you have the overwhelming feeling that they can peer into your head too. And by no means did I want anyone peeking just now into the swarm of thoughts that kept swirling around.

I had been sitting there for about ten minutes in a pose like a parody of Rodin's "Thinker" who is having a tough time of it, when an SMS arrived. *Important news*—the inspector wrote me, politely avoiding a phone call while I was in this place. I got up, raised the lid, flushed for no reason, then waited a bit so as to leave the impression I was adjusting my clothes and washing my hands. My phone rang as I came out.

"What happened?" I inquired.

"A big turnabout," the inspector said. Since we had begun talking, this was the first time her voice had indicated that she was upset. "There are no doubles."

"They didn't show up?" I proposed in bewilderment as I went to the study.

"They did, and they didn't."

"What do you mean?"

"They appeared on the screens in the control room, but not in reality. Our people in the field didn't see anyone."

"But that's not possible. They must have been confused. They didn't see things properly. How many look-alikes appeared on the screen altogether?"

"Two. My colleagues weren't confused. They saw everything. They even recorded what they saw with their cell phones. In the recordings, there is no one in the places where we clearly saw the avatars of Ms. Đurić on the screens."

"I don't understand…"

"What's happening is clear. How it's happening is not."

"Nothing is clear to me…" I said as I sat down at the desk.

"Someone has managed to master our surveillance system. They're showing something that, in fact, is not there."

"Is it possible to make it so realistic?"

"Obviously it is. Right now, we're checking the recordings. Everything still seems perfectly authentic."

"Who is behind this? This can hardly be the work of ordinary hackers, though you did tell me that nowadays anyone can do special effects."

"Not this special. For this, you have to be a specialist hacker."

"Specialist?"

"Yes. This is far beyond the amateur level. You need professional equipment, complex logistics, good protection. And that can be offered only by someone powerful. A country, for instance. This could easily be an attack by state-run hackers."

I felt like giving a whistle. "Which country could be behind the attacks?"

"Do we, like everyone else, have so few enemies? Not to mention our supposed friends…"

"Just awful. What are they trying to achieve by attacking our police surveillance system?"

"Who knows? Maybe nothing right away. It could be that they're just clandestinely preparing the ground for cyber-sabotage in case of a conflict in the near or further future. That's being done all over the world."

"Clandestinely? But here they have revealed themselves. The sabotage is ongoing right now."

"Yes, that's a bit unusual. Maybe it happened accidentally. If you hadn't reported Ms. Đurić missing last night, they probably would have gone unnoticed."

"Maybe the conflict has already started. An unannounced cyber-war…"

"Nothing is to be excluded, although it's probably something else. Certain terrorist organizations are more powerful than many countries. They are also capable of pulling off something like this."

"A terrorist attack on Belgrade?"

"For example."

"What do you plan to do?" Even though I was trying to remain calm, my voice betrayed me.

"The municipal police are insufficient to handle a terrorist attack. We have been joined by some of the other agencies, better equipped than us."

"The National Security Agency?"

"Among others."

"But what can you do if your surveillance system has been compromised? Virtual Ivana is popping up all over the place…"

"We will have to turn it off, but not right away. Let them go on thinking that we haven't discovered them yet. Fortunately, it's not the only such system, so we won't be left without surveillance. Another one has already been activated. We'll know exactly what is happening, no matter what they serve up to us on the first one."

"How many surveillance systems do you have?" I asked in disbelief.

"Every agency has its own, of course. Regarding Ms. Đurić, our colleagues from other agencies are very interested in why the possible terrorists chose her precisely to, as you say, pop up all over the place. That certainly cannot be a coincidence. One of them will probably call to talk to you soon."

"I am glad to hear it. It will give me an opportunity to ask them—where is Ivana? What are they going to do to find her? You spent a long time convincing me that she had gone last night to that mysterious building with eight apartments. But what if your surveillance system was already under the influence of terrorists or a state-run hacker or whatever? We don't actually know anything for certain about what happened to Ivana after she left the apartment in the early evening. It is quite possible that they kidnapped her then and have done who knows what to her in the meantime."

"Yet, the question remains—why her? And searching for an answer, my colleagues won't first assume that Ms. Đurić has been abducted and that something happened to her afterwards; they will rather suppose that she herself is a terrorist. It's a much simpler and more probable explanation."

"Nonsense!" I shouted. "Terrorist indeed! Ivana is the most harmless being I ever met! I have been living with her long enough to know that quite well. You will just go on wasting time on that ridiculous presumption. If you had listened to me, you could have started searching for her last night instead of…"

"And from Ms. Đurić," the inspector broke in, "it's only a step to you."

"To me?" I was shocked.

"At the height of a terrorist attack, the main suspect floods you with impossible links which lead to enigmatic videos. You claim that you don't see any meaning in them, but that is hard to believe. You'd claim the same thing if you were a part of the terrorist conspiracy, no? Perhaps you are the one pulling the strings…"

"Have you lost your mind?" I shrieked again. "I am the one who reported everything to you; if it weren't for me, you would have no idea about the terrorist attack—you said so yourself just now. You know quite well that I have not been in contact with anyone except you since last night. I am right in front of your eyes all the time, you filled my apartment with cameras. I agreed to cooperate with you. And now, suddenly, I am a terrorist leader who…" I didn't manage to finish the sentence because out of excitement I lost my voice.

As opposed to mine, the inspector's voice was completely calm. "Whatever the case, we come back to two key problems. What is Ms. Đurić doing in all this, and what do the videos she's sending you mean? Until we answer those questions, we have no one else to suspect apart from the two of you."

"Very well then," I responded, my voice still quivering. "Find Ivana and she will clarify everything for you, I am convinced. You will thereby also do me a big favor."

"Oh, we will, don't worry. It is no longer a question of manpower, authorization, and other trivialities. The country's in danger and all agencies are on high alert. We will find Ms. Đurić even if we have to turn over every stone."

"Excellent," I uttered breathlessly, and this time I hung up.

Sitting at my desk, I put down my phone, pulled off my glasses, closed my eyes, and put my face in my hands. There was drumming in my ears, pounding in my temples. I dared not even think of how high my blood pressure was. Honestly, to suspect that I was the culprit behind some sort of terrorist action...

Please, Ivana, come back—I cried out in my head. Whatever was going on, now it had been enough. I could not take any more. Since last night, I had been under constant stress, and I had not had a break since this morning. If this went on, I was a dead man. Even had I been younger, it would have been difficult, and how much more so at the age of seventy-three.

Suddenly, an exit from the hopelessness occurred to me. Genius in its childish simplicity. I would turn off all the lights in the apartment, go to the bedroom, stretch out fully clothed on the bed, and then simply— go to sleep. If they came to arrest me, they would not be able to wake me up. That is how hard I would be sleeping. Let them take me off to prison. I would not wake up there either—not until tomorrow at least. Then we would see what happened…

I put on my glasses and reached out to start turning off the lights with the one on the desk, but halfway there, I was stopped by a gong. I hesitated for a few seconds, then sighed. It was pointless. I had entered the dance, and now I would have to keep going to the end. But at least not by the rules imposed. I grabbed the mouse and forthwith clicked on the so-called link, not giving the police a chance to see the new video first. Or some other agency, it made no difference. Our cooperation had come to an end.

A smallish locale was illuminated by a dim reddish light. The tone was set by the lamps with dark red shades on four small round tables. Each had three chairs with arched wooden backs. In the background there was also a small bar. This was most likely a bistro or perhaps a teashop.

Upon each table were also partitioned porcelain dishes. The sections were full of something that looked to me like twigs, or berries of various colors. On one table was a rounded black vessel like a teapot, and three largeish cups and saucers.

Ivana entered at the twelfth second. She stopped briefly at the entrance, probably waiting for her eyes to adjust to the dim lighting, then went over to the coat rack in the corner and hung her umbrella on it. Then she sat down at the table with the teapot and placed her purse on the chair to the left.

Turning briefly towards the bar, she lifted the round lid from the teapot. A wisp of steam curled out of the vessel. She quickly replaced the lid, then pulled the dish with the multi-colored ingredients towards her. First she looked them all over with a smile, then picked it up and sniffed the items in each section.

She put the dish back on the table, took the teapot by its handle and half-filled the nearest cup with hot liquid. As the steam rose from it, she began adding ingredients with a teaspoon. First dark stems, then ochre granules, bluish flakes, orange powder, and brown sprinkles. She stirred for a while until the mixture turned dark green.

Even though the cup must have been hot, she did not pick it up by the handle, but rather cupped it in her hands. She brought it to her mouth, blew on it a little, then took a sip. She kept it in her mouth to check the taste, like someone tasting wine. Evidently satisfied, she finally swallowed it, before continuing to sip the spiced tea slowly until it was all gone.

It did not confuse me so much that Ivana managed to drink without discomfort the steaming beverage which must have burned her mouth. What seemed even more improbable was that, while normally never adding anything at all to her tea, she was now enjoying a variety of ingredients that together had who knows what kind of taste.

Setting the cup on the table, she got up, took her purse, and set off in the direction opposite the door. It seemed she was heading straight into the wall until she drew quite close. Only then did I detect something which had previously remained hidden in the dim lighting: there was some sort of dark red drapery there. She went through it, then her hand reappeared from behind the curtain and she waved to me.

The scene froze at two minutes and seven seconds.

27

My cell phone rang as soon as I closed the video window. I let it ring. I stared at the dark screen framed with series of icons along all four edges. Ivana once told me that the orderly appearance of my home screen was a proper mirror of my personality. She did not answer my question as to whether that was praise or reproof. It seemed to me that the home screen on her laptop was the embodiment of disorder, to which she replied that she liked it exactly that way. What could I say to that?

I answered after the eleventh ring. I expected a reprimand, but it did not come. The inspector got right down to business, as if she were tacitly admitting her measure of blame for the raised voices in our previous conversation.

"This is the teashop from *The Last Book*, isn't it?"

I raised my eyebrows. "Where did you get that idea?"

"The reddish dim light, the four small tables, the dishes with various additions to tea... The only thing missing was that little Oriental guy speaking funny broken Serbian."

"It just seems so to you. Teashops all look mostly alike. Especially Oriental ones."

"This is precisely how I imagined the one you described in the novel."

"I did not imagine it that way."

"How did you then?"

I did not reply straight away. "Differently…"

"That doesn't tell me much. How so, differently?"

"Does that really matter right now? I think we have more important business than dealing with how I imagined a teashop."

"To be fair, it's not impossible that I don't remember it well," the inspector continued, paying no heed to my comment. "It's been several years since I read *The Last Book*. Soon I'll go back to remind myself exactly how you described it. I just acquired the digital versions of all your books."

"I'm quite flattered, but I still don't think this is the right moment for us to analyze the finesses in *The Last Book*."

"It's not just about *The Last Book*."

"Rather?"

"I have to check something in your other works as well. Especially in those I haven't read yet."

"What do you want to check? Why?"

The inspector avoided answering. "It's a pity that I didn't attend your creative writing classes, Professor Živković…"

"It's never too late for that. Enroll as soon as this is over. Hopefully, the investigation will accelerate now with the new manpower. Is there any news?"

"I don't know."

"What do you mean, you don't know?" I asked after a brief pause.

"The municipal police have been taken off the case. It's been taken over by other agencies. We're just lending them technical support."

"What do I do now? Who will keep me informed?"

"No one. I've been harshly reprimanded because I have been reporting the progress of the case until now.

The lead suspect is never informed about the ongoing investigation."

"But I am not... I cannot be... the lead suspect..."

"Unfortunately, you are. Together with Ms. Đurić. Until something changes..."

"Are they going to arrest me?"

"I don't know. I don't believe so. They have you under complete surveillance. You're easily available to them. It's more or less like you've already been arrested. You could be of more use to them at large."

"That's a very small 'at large'."

"Even that's a lot better than confinement."

"Will they tell me when... if... they find Ivana?"

"Probably not right away..."

"Then when?"

"After they interrogate her. That could last a while..."

"Should I find her a lawyer now?"

"She won't be allowed a lawyer. This is no longer a normal police investigation. We are in an unannounced state of emergency. National security is in danger."

"Just awful. What an ordinary disappearance has given birth to..."

"A quite extraordinary one..."

"Won't they reprimand you again for talking to me now?"

"They haven't forbidden that. I just can't inform you about the progress of the investigation. Anyway, our conversations are all being recorded."

"Are the... injunctions... still in place? I can't leave the apartment, I shouldn't be near the window..."

"Everything remains the same. Until you get new instructions."

"I still have to wait while you look at the new record-ings first?"

"Only that you no longer have to do. They are now using better equipment than ours."

We fell silent briefly.

"Why did you acquire the digital editions of my books?" I was the first to break the silence. "What do you wish to check in them?"

"I'll tell you after I've checked. It could take a while. You've written a lot of books, Professor Živković."

"I shall take that as a compliment. Perhaps I could help you accelerate your research."

"Thank you. I'll let you know if I get stuck. We'll be in touch."

I put the phone down on the desk and remained seated. I had already become somewhat accustomed to the previous surveillance. I had grown familiar with at least one person watching my every step. Now, however, I was being eyed by complete strangers. I was overcome with discomfort, as if I had been publicly undressed.

I probably would have gone on sitting there unobtrusively doing nothing if I had not suddenly been hit by an attack of yawning. Until two or three years earlier, I had had no empathy for those who took daytime naps. It seemed like a waste of time to me. Then I myself gradually began to realize the usefulness of short afternoon naps. Especially on those days when I held creative writing classes. Twenty minutes of deep dreamless sleep would be quite refreshing for the upcoming two-hour effort.

Today I first tried to cover my yawns, as I would do if I were in the company of someone (and I was in someone's company, but in a very special way); then I realized that a short rest now, actually, would be useful on several counts. Above all, it would offer me a valuable break in one of the most strenuous and stressful days I had ever lived through; who knew what other excitements awaited me in the evening or however long this whole thing was going to last. In addition, I would not, at least briefly, have to worry about making a bad move in the eyes of those now watching me. I would probably look comical to them while I was asleep—I often did to Ivana—but that was the least of my worries right now.

I headed for the living room and put my cell phone on the end table, then stretched out on the couch. I put two cushions under my head and turned towards the back. Sleep overcame me, it seemed, the instant I closed my eyes. As did waking. I had the feeling I had not slept at all, but a look at my cell phone convinced me otherwise: 5:32 PM. I had spent a good quarter hour in a coma. As usual, I was quite groggy, so it took some time for me to wake up enough to ask the question: what made me wake up so quickly? I did not have to look long for the answer. It was as if the echoes of the computer notification were still in my ears.

I went back to the study, sat at the desk, put the phone under the monitor, and opened the e-mail window. At the end of the long series, Ivana's seventeenth e-mail awaited me. Clicking immediately on the "link", I thought it was not all bad coming under the authority of the secret services that stand above the police. At least you didn't have to wait in line to look at a video sent to you.

One could tell right away it was a fancy restaurant. Period furniture, thick carpeting, large paintings with engraved frames. The tables set with luxurious place settings: silver and crystal. The menus in dark brown leather covers. One table stood apart. In the center of it rose a rather large roll-shaped form, with a domed upper part and a thick ring at the top. One could not tell what it was because it was completely draped in a thick black velvet cover.

Ivana came into the frame from somewhere on the left at the eighth second. She turned briefly and sort of curtsied, with a smile, to someone behind her. Then she went to the special table. She put her purse on a chair set there, her umbrella on another, then walked around the round table looking at the upright black cylinder from all angles. Finally she sat down on a third chair.

She reached out and pulled a black ribbon with a tassel on the end, which I had previously missed. The cover slid down, and a cage appeared. It sparkled yellow, as if its bars were made of gold. Inside, there was not a single bird, but I was rendered breathless nonetheless. I had never seen such luxuriant bird feathers as those covering the bottom of the cage, flaring in all the colors of the rainbow.

Ivana opened the cage door, put her hand inside and dug into the feathers. She plucked about them for a time, obviously enjoying the almost sensual touch. Then she pulled out a handful of small feathers. Some of them fell away as she pulled her hand across the table. When she drew it close, she opened her fist turned downwards and let the downy load fall gently on a large porcelain plate in front of her.

She pulled off her beret and began sticking feathers in tiny holes in the back of it. I had not even known they were there. Ten-odd quills stood straight up, turning the cap into a small aigrette. She put the beret back on, stood up and approached a large mirror between two pictures on a nearby wall. There, she fluffed up and adjusted the feathers. Satisfied, she turned to the camera high on the opposite wall and waved at me with a smile.

She remained frozen in that position, while in the corner of the screen stood 1:36. The scene looked incredible, but not so much because of the bird of paradise feathers. Ivana, who fiercely defended animal rights, would never ornament herself with the remains of a living being, no matter how beautiful they were.

28

As I CLOSED THE video window, it occurred to me that an entire day had just passed since the last time I'd seen Ivana. Like yesterday, I turned away from the screen towards the door of the study. She was standing there, dressed to go out; she did not say anything to my inquisitive look, she just smiled and waved at me. How could I have guessed then what was awaiting me?

Here I was now in the same place, only twenty-four hours later; Ivana had disappeared without a trace, I was under house arrest, the secret services were watching my every move, we were both suspected of preparing a terrorist attack and the enigmas around me just kept multiplying.

And that was not all. Who knew what else would happen, how long it would all last, and how it would all end? To one of these three questions I had, in fact, already guessed the answer, even though I pretended that nothing was clear to me. If it went on like this, the final act—whatever it might be—was to come in something less than two and a half hours. There were only five of Ivana's e-mails to go—five more videos—and they arrived at intervals of half an hour. (Only the first two, for some reason, had been separated by an hour.)

I had only gradually recognized the thread connecting the recordings, but I was keeping that insight to myself. I had assured the inspector that I did not see any sense in the videos because I wanted to conceal what it was that tied Ivana's messages together. Without that connection, nothing was involving me in a case which was becoming more complex and unpleasant with each new message. I could pretend that none of this was related to me at all, except that, of course, it was really important to me that Ivana be found as soon as possible.

Now, however, the inspector had also begun linking the recordings together, and it no longer made sense to go on pretending. It would seem like she knew my opus better than I did, and that should not be allowed to happen. Not only would it be unconvincing, but it would also bring my honor as an author into question.

Each video introduced a scene from one of my books. Only the first was for some reason outside, while the other sixteen were in an interior, mostly in a particular room. The books had been laid out chronologically— from the first, *The Fourth Circle*, to the seventeenth, *Escher's Loops*. There were five left—from *The Ghost-writer* to *The Image Interpreter*.

Five books, five videos, something less than two and a half hours…

I had not realized that in the first one was the jungle from *The Fourth Circle*. In fact, I did notice the dark yellow blur through the thick undergrowth at the very end of the video, but how could I have recognized the wall of a Buddhist temple from that?

In the second video, hidden from my view were the two things that would have clued me into the atelier of the mentally ill painter from the final part of *Time Gifts*: black cloth covered three pictures on the wall, and the large, barred window through which light poured in was outside the scope of the camera.

The desk in the third video had led me down the wrong path. It seemed to be the desk from my former study. I did not remember at first that I had described the desk in *The Writer* after the example of my own desk from the period when I was writing that book.

It had first occurred to me that the enactment of scenes from a literary work was going on when I saw the fourth video. As if I had read somewhere about some kind of auction in just such surroundings. As I watched the video, however, it did not cross my mind that it was an episode from my novel *The Book*.

I finally recognized my own work in the fifth video, as I was freezing on the park bench, even though the recording deviated from its literary forerunner: in the first story of *Impossible Encounters*, there was just one butterfly, while the video included a whole swarm. Yet, despite this difference, I immediately realized what I was seeing.

After that, it all went more easily. First I recognized my own work in the previous videos, realized in which order they were appearing, and on the basis of that, knew which novel or collection of stories would be presented in the upcoming videos.

The sixth took place in the garret from the last story in *Seven Touches of Music*, the seventh in the studio from the second story in *The Library*, the eighth in the classroom from the introductory story to *Steps Through the Mist*, the ninth in the secondhand bookstore in *Hidden Camera*, the tenth in the first-class compartment in *Compartments*, the eleventh in the hotel room in the third part of *Four Stories till the End*, the twelfth in the pastry shop from the first story in *Twelve Collections*, the thirteenth in the small room with a barrel from the third part of *The Bridge*, the fourteenth in the museum from the fourth story in *Miss Tamara, the Reader*, the fifteenth in the antique store from the second story in *Amarcord*, the sixteenth in the teashop in *The Last Book*, and the seventeenth in the fancy restaurant in *Escher's Loops*.

Even though it had taken me some time to figure out what Ivana was showing me, this was still the easier part. In all other respects, I was still fumbling around in the impenetrable dark. I did not even have a hunch about why she had chosen these parts of the books, these surroundings, and not others. It was as if there was no common denominator amongst them, or I was unable to see it. The only thing connecting them was something not related to the books themselves but to Ivana, who appeared there as a sort of foreign entity: there was always some feature of hers that diverged from what I knew for certain about her. As if those traits were constantly indicating that, in fact, it was not her, which made no sense whatsoever.

An even more important question was why she was doing all this. If she wanted to tell me something about my books, there were far simpler ways she could do that, without causing so much trouble to us both. It occurred to me that she had not even figured that the things she had come up with might spin out of control and ultimately reach the secret services and a state of emergency. Maybe she thought I would not report her disappearance to the police. If I had not done so, all of this would now be just between her and me. But how could I not report her missing? How could she think that I would sit on my hands and wait for all of this to somehow resolve on its own? Would she have done that if I had gone missing?

And most importantly—what was it, actually, that

she was trying to tell me? What was it that justified getting involved in such a far-reaching, complex, and risky undertaking? Not to mention the expense of it, no matter whether it was the staging of a multitude of surroundings, or resorting to professional special effects. Was it possible that behind it all stood Ivana's feeling of insult because I had reproached her in passing that she had not read all of my books, and her now investing enormous effort and money (which she did not have anyway) to show me that not only had she read all of them, but also probed them more profoundly than I, thus managing to connect them in a way that I couldn't make any sense of?

However, Ivana was neither that sensitive nor vain, even less so vengeful. This kind of thing was not like her at all. And if it had been, she simply did not have the means or money to execute an undertaking of such magnitude. But if that were so, what then, actually, was going on? Who was pulling the strings of everything that had happened to me since last night, and why? What was Ivana's role in it all? What was even happening to her? The entire situation, unless I was wrong, was drawing to an end, but I was still at the beginning, in the absolute dark. All I could do was sit here and wait to see what would happen to me next.

Ivana's eighteenth e-mail found me next. When the gong sounded behind my back, I turned away from the door towards the monitor and first looked at the clock in the lower right corner: 6.00. Right on time. Whoever was pulling the strings, they were doing so with precision.

As I slid the cursor towards the new "link", I realized that I had not heard from the inspector between Ivana's two messages. She must be intent on her search through the digital version of my books. She was fortunate that it exists, otherwise she would have had to spend weeks reading the fiction works of a writer who had reached the limit when it comes to scribomania...

In *The Ghostwriter*, there is only one setting, so there was no choice. I saw what I had imagined as a combination of several of my studies which differed only insignificantly: walls covered with full bookshelves, a large desk with the usual writer's inventory, a small couch, an armchair and a coffee table between them, three picture windows full of sunlight. If the bright external light were taken away, the scene on the screen would have been almost the same as the one surrounding me.

Ivana had entered earlier than usual this time, already by the fifth second. She put her purse and umbrella on the larger of two taborets, and began walking around the room. She lightly ran her hand over the surfaces of things as she passed them. She stopped a little longer next to the desk. Resting on her forearms on the back of the desk chair, she turned towards the camera above the door and waved at me with a smile. Then she went over to the armchair and sat down.

The sound I then heard was so unexpected that, at first, I thought I had imagined it. Then the rough purring repeated itself, and from behind the couch Felix's large head appeared. Buca's head. A lump came to my throat, and my eyes welled up. I was glad that Ivana could not see me. I had never cried in front of her.

I have a lot of photos of Buca, but not a single video. The memories of my favorite cat, in whose company I wrote the major portion of my books, were quite vivid, but to see him moving around live was something more than a memory. He headed towards the armchair with his usual limping walk. He stopped at Ivana's feet, sniffed her, checking to make certain, then hopped up into her lap before I was able to warn him not to do so. And if I had, what good would it have done? Ivana is not only allergic to strawberries. She is even more bothered by cat and dog hair.

But instead of backing off or jumping out of the chair, she began to pet Buca down the length of his back. The scene was completely surreal. The cat's purring became stuttering, like the sound of a somewhat impotent little engine. Then something even more unbelievable happened. Ivana leaned down and kissed Buca where I would most joyfully have done: between the ears.

The two heads remained frozen one above the other when the recording ended at the forty-seventh second.

∽ 29 ∾

I LEFT THE VIDEO window open on this final scene.
The excitement of seeing Buca again slowly subsided
in me, even though I knew from the very beginning,
of course, that the recording was not real. It could not
have been. He and Ivana had never been together. And
there was still not a single video with my cat.

Ivana's eighteenth e-mail finally removed any doubt
whether the videos were staged settings from my books
or special effects. Everything else could have been real
except Buca. Even if they had found a complete feline
double for him, it would not have been able to copy his
unique purring or his gait. It was a virtual Buca, but
his appearance still excited me just as much as if I had
seen the real one who had come alive by some miracle.

As I wiped with my forefingers the dampness behind
the lower part of my glasses, my telephone rang.

"That's exactly how I imagined Felix," the inspector
said.

"Buca," I corrected her.

"Yeah, Buca. He was still alive while you were writing *The Ghostwriter*, right?"

"Oh, yes. Very much so. He died five years later, in
2014. You have read *The Ghostwriter* too?"

"I've read exactly half your books. If it weren't so, I
never would have thought that the videos were scenes
from your work." She paused briefly. "You could've

spared me from searching through the digital editions. You knew from the beginning what the videos were showing. Why didn't you tell me?"

"Does this mean you are back on the case?" I avoided answering her.

"I never left it. I'm not the lead any longer, but I haven't been forbidden from working on it. Again, why didn't you tell me?"

"I didn't know from the beginning. It took me some time before I realized it..."

"You didn't immediately recognize things that you had thought up?"

"I already mentioned it to you with the teashop from *The Last Book*. What I imagined doesn't always match what we see in the videos. It's different..."

"All right, as you say. Why didn't you tell me when you finally realized what was in the videos?"

"Because then you would draw the incorrect conclusion that I was involved in all this. You were already doing so anyway. Would you have believed that I had no idea why Ivana was sending me recordings of places from my books, and why she had chosen them and not others?"

"That would be tough to believe."

"There, you see."

A moment passed before the inspector spoke again.

"Are you writing anything new right now, Professor Živković?"

Now I hesitated before answering.

"Why does that interest you?"

"No reason. I'm just curious. You don't have to tell me if it's a secret."

"It is not. I am not writing anything new. I have more than enough of the old. Did you not reprimand me for writing so many books?"

"It was not a reprimand. I'm sorry if it sounded like that."

"You were entirely right, actually. Twenty-two books really is a lot. And five years have passed now since my last novel came out. I have gotten rusty as a writer. Also, I don't feel much like writing at the moment. You see yourself what headaches it brings."

"You think that this is related to your writing?"

"Well, it revolves around it at least partially, judging from the videos, right?"

"Yes. Maybe. I read in one of your interviews... You talked about your writing method. Very interesting. About how at the beginning you don't know what you will write about, then you start capturing it like some sort of dictation... from your subconscious... if I understood you well."

"Something like that."

"Really unusual."

"Actually, it isn't rare for a writer to work that way."

"And you really don't know at the start what you'll write about?"

"It isn't that I do not know at all. I have a certain notion. It is like through the fog I see a beacon towards which I am sailing. The fog dissipates as the writing advances..."

"And in that... unconscious... the work already exists, complete, even before you sit down to write? It pressures you to let it out...?"

"That is all a metaphor..."

"What will you do if you feel that pressure again?"

"Good question. I don't know. I'm not sure that I really need a twenty-third book..."

"Do you think you could stop it from coming out?"

I shrugged. "I don't know that either. I have never

tried. Until now, I have always given in to the pressure..."

"It's not easy being a writer," said the inspector with a smile in her voice.

"Tell me about it," I responded likewise in a cheerful tone. "You seem quite interested in the writer's call. Do you perhaps have a wish to try your hand at writing too?"

"Me? No, no. I don't have a gift for it. My mind is different. Without that... unconscious..."

"We all have an unconscious."

It seemed to me that she mumbled "unfortunately", but I was not sure. I did not ask her to repeat herself because we had already strayed fairly far from the subject. She should enroll in my course if she wished to discuss such topics.

"I would ask you to do me a favor," I said with some hesitation. "I know that they are listening to and recording our conversation, but it doesn't matter. Would you please inform me when they find Ivana? Just that, nothing more. Just so I can know that she is all right. That surely won't interfere with the investigation."

"We'll talk soon, Professor Živković," she gave an indefinite answer after a brief silence.

I closed the video window with Ivana and Buca, and rose from the desk. I put my palms on my lower back and stretched. I felt as stiff as if I had spent the whole day continuously in front of the computer, when, in fact, I had gotten up fairly often. If someone had been with me in the study, I would have restrained myself from stretching, of course, but I didn't have to pay much attention to courtesy in front of those watching me from afar. My life would become fairly unbearable if I had constantly to take heed and not appear impolite in the eyes of those who were monitoring me day and night.

Just as I relaxed my hands, I was stopped short by a thought. It was Wednesday, at seven-thirty I had a yoga class over Skype. In the general chaos that governed my day, I had completely forgotten about it. I would not even have remembered it now if I had not stretched. There was no way I could attend class; I needed to inform the instructor about it immediately. I sent Olja an SMS, and resolved that I could also exercise briefly without the class, until something else extraordinary happened. It would feel good to loosen up a little.

As I laid out the pink mat in its usual place on the floor in front of my desk, I wondered if I should put on my sweats as I usually did for yoga. Maybe it was better after all to remain dressed the way I was, I concluded. I would not overdo it, so I would not sweat, if I just got moving with some light stretches on the floor. And who knows how the agencies would view my changing clothes. It might seem like I was defying them by exercising in sweats in the middle of a state of emergency for which they held me partly accountable. Though, of course, I felt no guilt whatsoever, it would still be better not to offend them.

I was in the middle of the third position when the gong sounded. I executed it to the end, and only then got up off the floor. There was no hurry. Before I sat in front of the monitor, I rolled up the mat, returned it to its place, and straightened my clothes a bit.

I immediately recognized the luxurious Vienna salon from the second part of *The Five Wonders of the Danube*, though there it is seen briefly and through a keyhole. There could be no mistake: only there in the middle of the room did a pyramid of books rise, above which was hanging a noose at the end of a rope tied to a hook in the high ceiling.

Ivana entered at the seventh second. She put her umbrella and purse on the antique chair just left of the door and approached the pyramid. At first, she just observed it, as if marveling at a museum piece, then she began to go around and look at it carefully from all sides. She would stop here and there to read the title on the spine of a book.

After coming full circle, she pulled off her black ankle boots, then looked at the camera and nodded at me with a smile. Everything that happened after that was completely uncharacteristic of her. The Ivana I knew would never stand on a book; she would never clamber up on something as unstable as this hillock of stacked books; even less, once she reached the top, would she get up on her tiptoes, grab the noose, and start swinging while letting out cries of happiness, like a child enjoying itself in the park.

I watched in disbelief as her swaying body described an ever greater arc. If she went on like this, she would soon inevitably slam into the ceiling in front or in back. Yet this did not happen. She abruptly let go of the noose, like a gymnast dismounting after a ring exercise. Carried by inertia, she flew with her feet forwards, but there was no landing. The video ended at the fifty-fifth second.

It was most unusual to see Ivana in a flying pose—Ivana who otherwise thought that, for her taste, even those exercises I execute at yoga training while lying on a mat were too dynamic.

30

I closed the video window. Dressed in her overcoat and shoeless, almost horizontally stretched just beneath the ceiling, Ivana looked comical, but I did not feel like laughing. Since there were only three more videos with locations from my last three books still to come, some sort of denouement was imminent, and it would hardly be cheerful, considering where we had got to since the night before.

The case was being run by several secret agencies, I was under house arrest which could easily become actual or something worse, there was not a trace of Ivana anywhere, nor was it known what her role in all of this was. Could I possibly hope for something good to happen in the end?

I got up from the desk and went to wash my hands, a little late, from my exercises on the floor. I left the bathroom door open so as not to rouse suspicion amongst those watching me, if indeed there were no cameras in there. It would be useful to let them know at every opportunity that they could still count on me to cooperate.

I stopped at the bathroom door, indecisive about how to fill the time until Ivana's next video. I was even less in the mood than previously to go on reading Binet's novel. Perhaps I could watch television for a little while. I am certainly not one of those who, not knowing what to do with themselves, waste valuable time channel-surfing. At the moment, however, that actually seemed attractive; to numb myself a bit with something silly and turn my thoughts away from everything.

I went into the living room, picked up the remote, sat on the couch and pressed the green button. The picture should have appeared after five or six seconds, but the screen remained dark. I looked at the center of the lower edge of the black television frame; a small circle appears there when the television is on. It was shining milk-white, which meant that the batteries in the remote were all right; my first thought was that they had died, since it had happened more than once that I could not turn on the television because the batteries were dead.

I changed the channel, but there was still no picture. I pressed the channel button several more times—again without effect. This could only mean one thing: for some reason, I was getting no signal from the provider. That did not worry me at first. Occasionally it happened that I did not have a picture for a short while. Providers are not perfect. Actually, it was better this way. I would find something smarter than television to entertain myself with.

Then, however, I remembered that I received my Internet along with my television signal from the same provider. If there was no picture, then the Internet connection was also down. I almost jumped off the couch and hurried back to the study. I leaned in close to the lower right corner of the monitor because the little icons there are really tiny. The one for the Internet was crossed out.

I grabbed my telephone from the desk and turned on

the screen. Even though I knew there would be no sign of Wi-Fi, I still cursed to myself when I got the confirmation. Why was such bad luck striking me now? As soon as this was over, I would change providers first thing. I was already touching the telephone screen to inform the inspector of my troubles when I was halted by a sudden thought.

What if this interruption was not the provider's fault at all? What if those now running the case had caused it? It surely wouldn't be difficult for them to do so. But why would they do that? To hinder me from watching the last three videos? What sense did that make? Anyway, I didn't need home Internet to do so. I also had it on my phone. I had already watched one video on my phone, on the bench in the park. The picture, true enough, was small, but big enough if necessary. But what if they remembered that I could watch them that way, too, and shut off my cell phone as well?

I didn't have the chance to delve into this question because my phone rang at that very moment.

"I don't have Internet anymore," I informed the inspector without introduction.

"I know."

"Why was it shut off?"

"I don't know."

I waited a moment for her to say more, but she obviously had no intention of elucidating.

"So what now?" I tried to extract more from her anyway.

She ignored my question. "You haven't been honest with me, Professor Živković."

"How so?"

"You told me that you weren't writing anything new."

"And I am not."

"Yet you've tried several times."

I hesitated briefly. "I did not."

"Yes, you did. You wrote several sentences. Once even three paragraphs."

"That doesn't count. False starts. I erased those little files. How do you even know they existed?"

"Files don't disappear when you erase them." She paused briefly. "Manuscripts don't burn."

"How do they not disappear?"

"It only seems that they're gone, but they're still on your hard drive. You can get them back if you know how."

I remained silent for a few moments, then spoke out more quietly than before. "You hacked my computer?"

As a reflex, as if protecting myself from an attack, I grabbed the mouse and moved the cursor to the lower left corner of the screen to turn the computer off.

"You don't have to do that. Now you're safe from hacking. You're no longer online. And we didn't hack you."

Just one click away from turning off the computer, I stopped. "Then how do you know what I erased?"

"We copied the contents of your entire hard drive when we were at your place."

My face flushed. "How dare you? You had no ri…" I gurgled and lost my voice.

"Calm down, Professor Živković. Nothing terrible happened. First of all, we had the right to check your hard drive. We got a warrant for it. Besides, we'll erase everything we copied as soon as the case ends. The law obliges us to."

"As if you cared about the law…"

"Much more than you think."

"If any of my private data from the hard drive ever appears on the Internet, no one will be able to protect you. I will sue you and will not desist until I reach the highest courts. We shall go before the international courts if needed…"

"Rest assured, nothing will leak onto the Internet from us."

I took a deep breath, then exhaled, trying to calm down a bit.

"All of that just to pluck out a couple of useless erased files…"

"Maybe they're not useless."

"What can be useful about several sentences in which a former author unnecessarily and unsuccessfully attempts to begin one more book?"

"Not just any writer, but the author of *The Papyrus Trilogy*."

I stared at the screen, frowning, as if I could see the inspector's face in it.

"What difference does that make?"

Once again, she did not answer me. "Do you know how I came across that trilogy of yours?"

The question was, of course, only rhetorical. How could I know that?

"A colleague of mine recommended it to me. He's a big fan of yours. He even gave me a copy of the book to convince me to read it. Nevertheless, it lay unopened for months on my nightstand."

"There, that is the kind of humiliation awaiting you if you yourself set out to be a writer."

"But once I opened it before going to sleep, I didn't close it till, just before dawn, I finished the first part—*The Last Book*."

"Such compliments obliterate all the humiliations…"

"The end completely astounded me."

"I am glad. There were many who were disappointed…"

"I am otherwise a rational, sensible person. I don't have much of a leaning for fantastic literature. Yet the idea of two realities that cross seemed to be perfectly convincing to me, quite possible…"

"I did all I could to make it seem so…"

"Not just in a literary sense."

"Rather?"

"Rather in reality. Why couldn't it really be like that? Why should there be only one reality?"

The questions this time were not only rhetorical. I was expected to give an answer.

"Perhaps… Under certain conditions, of course… In any case, we live in a time of wonders, do we not?"

She did not continue immediately. As if she were weighing my words, looking for something in them that was not there: a deeper meaning. I had said the first thing that came to mind, just to say something. It was vague enough not to disappoint her. A writer never dares to disappoint an appreciative reader, even when they understand him too literally…

"That was two and a half months ago," she returned to the subject. "After *The Papyrus Trilogy*, I read eight more of your books. They're all excellent, but I was hoping that the idea of crossing realities would appear in at least one more of them. Maybe there'll be something in the remaining eleven. Did you ever write about that again?"

I cleared my throat. "A writer should never repeat himself…"

Before she was able to respond to this, the impossible gong resounded from the computer. In confusion,

I checked the little Internet icon. It was no longer crossed out.

"The Internet is back!" I almost shouted.

"I know," the inspector said. "Just one more detail before you look at the new video. You named one of the files 'The White Room'. What does that mean?"

I shook my head. "To be honest, I have no idea. It just came to me like that…"

"From your unconscious?"

"I guess…"

She remained silent for several moments. "All right. We'll continue our conversation soon, Professor Živković."

I put my phone on the desk and hurried to click on the blue alphanumerical sequence. Something crossed my mind at that moment: it was as if the problem with the so-called link had been swept under the rug. It was simply taken for granted that Ivana's videos were available through them, and no one was even asking how any longer. Or perhaps they were asking and just not telling me about it.

If I had not known from which book the new setting was taken, it would have been considerably harder for me to understand what was being shown on screen. It was as if I were looking at the lighted interior of a box of undefined dimensions, set upright and lined with mirrors: it could be as small as a shoe box, or two stories tall. Seen from above, the opposing walls reflecting in each other created an illusion of infinity.

I realized that it was an elevator only a moment before one of the walls divided in half and turned into a door. Ivana did not enter immediately. I did not see her, but I could imagine her standing at the door and hesitating. She suffers from a mild form of claustrophobia. She takes the elevator only when absolutely necessary. At our place, she occasionally takes it up to the fifth floor, but she always takes the stairs down. One like this—covered in mirrors—was precisely the last kind of elevator she would step into.

Now, however, it was as if it did not bother her at all. She looked up at the ceiling for a second and waved at me with a smile. After the antique shop, this was the second occasion when she did not have anywhere to put down her umbrella and purse, so she held on to them. When the door became a wall again, she turned to the left and gently ran her fingers across the middle of the large glass surface. From the place she had touched, a round bulge appeared, like a red hockey puck. She pushed it and it melted into the mirror again.

For a good half minute, everything was peaceful. Ivana stood unmoving like a mannequin in a display window. When she did finally start moving, it was in a completely unexpected way. As if she had magically become weightless, she rose up from the floor seemingly without effort. She simply started hovering.

She opened her purse as if everything were quite as usual and took out some knitting materials: a ball of sky-blue yarn, two long needles, and the start of a knitting project. I had never seen her with anything like that in her hands. She got down to work skillfully, like a highly experienced knitter. The knitting advanced, as if enjoying the weightless state. After only fifteen-odd seconds, the beginnings of a scarf had already been knitted.

At that moment, I remembered that just recently, when winter had begun baring its fangs, she had told me that I could really use another scarf. Confused, I had asked her what for, when the one she had bought me at the beginning of October was quite enough. She answered me in her own style—concisely: "You need it." She never mentioned it again.

The video stopped at one minute and twenty-seven seconds.

31

I CLOSED THE VIDEO window. My gaze fell on the Internet icon; it was crossed out again. I looked at my cell phone screen; once again, there was no Wi-Fi, but the telephone network was still there. I wasn't yet cut off completely from the world. I remained at my desk, convinced that the inspector would call immediately. She had seemed quite anxious to continue our conversation.

I was pleased, of course, that she liked *The Papyrus Trilogy*, but not that apparently she saw in it something more than a literary work. Sometimes, I am contacted by readers who have experienced one of my books too literally—not as the product of imagination but as a sort of report on something real. It is almost impossible to convince such people otherwise. Hopefully, it would not be that way with Ms. Mrvaljević. She seemed to me to be just as a police inspector should be—a rational and clearheaded person. After all, that is exactly how she had described herself. However, I did not understand why just now, at the peak of this crisis, she found as significant the crossing of realities in *The Papyrus Trilogy*; nor could I guess where our conversation about it was heading. But OK, all would soon be clear.

Still, the minutes passed, and the inspector did not call. But my stomach did—its growling reminded me it was time for dinner. I picked up the phone, went into the kitchen, and opened the refrigerator. I took some yogurt, cheese, and tomato to the kitchen table, and broke off a hunk of baguette from the breadbox. I would eat here, not in the dining room. Ivana would reprove me for this; she thought the small rituals of family life were important, but she was not here and this was easier for me. At lunch I had kept up the formalities, but now there was no time for them.

My cell phone rang as soon as I returned the food to the refrigerator and placed the used dishes in the sink. I was grateful to the inspector for her consideration in allowing me to eat. She could have waited, in fact, for a couple more minutes so I could wash the plate, glass, knife and fork, but that would be pandering to my almost eccentric orderliness.

"You outsmarted me, Professor Živković. Congratulations!"

"I don't understand," I responded after a brief hesitation.

"I naïvely supposed that you would save your new writing onto your hard drive."

"I am not writing anything new. I told you that—don't you remember?"

"The stuff we undeleted was just a diversion, right? Several alleged short beginnings to create the impression that you were trying a little, then gave up. Clever."

"I have no idea what you are talking about."

"Maybe the only true thing was that title—*The White Room*. You were longing to toy with us a little more. To prove how superior you are. It's not enough that you've been dragging us around by the nose since last night."

"Ms. Mrvaljević…"

"You're saving the file in some other place," she broke in. "You're convinced that you hid it well. Only, you are underestimating us. Do you really think that we don't have ways of finding out from you where it is?"

"I'm sure you do. What was it you told me? 'If the police were still like that, do you think I would be working here?' You do not think, I hope, that I believed you? That would really be naïve."

"I wasn't trying to deceive you. I would never work for a police force that extracts confessions under duress. But this case is no longer in the hands of the police. It's being run by agencies that are not picky about the means they use to defend national security."

"All right, let's say that everything you imagine is correct. I am clandestinely writing a novel entitled *The White Room*. I do not keep the file on my hard drive but save it in some hidden place. For the love of God, how would that be a threat to our national security?"

"Isn't it obvious? What has happened in less than 24 hours? First, the so-called links showed up that no one can explain, and we sought help from all over the world. There's even a suggestion that we turn off the global Internet until this gets solved. Then, someone got into the impenetrable video surveillance system of the Belgrade police and played hide-and-seek with us, and there isn't the slightest trace of a hacker attack or internal sabotage. Finally, Ms. Đurić disappeared without a trace, and is sending you videos of herself from places in your books."

"Except for the last statement, what could all of that have to do with my writing?"

The inspector was silent for a few moments. "You already answered that question yourself, Professor Živković. In *The Papyrus Trilogy*."

"What did I answer?"

"Realities have crossed. Our reality and the reality of

your new novel. Writing it, you are pulling the strings of all the impossible things that are happening here."

I shook my head. "Insane…" I raised my voice slightly, "No one is pulling any strings. There is no sort of crossing of realities. That is just a quaint concept from a literary work…"

"How then would you explain all the impossible things happening to us?"

"I do not know. There must be some… reasonable… explanation…"

"Or we will have to change Sherlock Holmes's famous slogan. You remember, he mentioned it often: 'Once you eliminate the impossible, whatever remains, no matter how improbable, must be the truth.' The new version could be: 'Once you eliminate even improbable explanations, whatever remains, no matter how impossible, must be the truth.'"

Once again, I shook my head and repeated, "Insane…"

"*The White Room* is actually what is happening to us, right? How does it end?"

Again my voice intensified slightly. "*The White Room* does not exist. I am not hiding the file anywhere. I am not writing anything. I wanted to, but I simply could not. I am finished with writing. Please believe me about this."

This time, the inspector's silence lasted somewhat longer. When she did start speaking, her voice was quiet, unlike mine. "I still might be able to believe you, but I'm afraid that those who are now running the case couldn't do so even if they wanted to. If they did start believing you, they would be left without even impossible explanations, and for them that would be equal to defeat."

"When will they come for me?" I was almost whispering.

"I don't know. Soon, I suppose." She stopped for a moment. "If this were your novel after all, how would you save yourself?"

I shrugged. "I have no idea. It seems there is no way out. I would need some sort of *deus ex machina*..."

The sound of a gong rang out in the study.

"I hope there will be a chance for us to talk one more time, Professor Živković."

"I would be glad..."

I went back to my desk, put down the phone, clicked on the "link" because of which the whole world might soon be left without the Internet for a while.

The space that showed up on the monitor was not small, but it seemed a little tight because the walls were completely covered with glass-fronted shelves filled with dark gray volumes of equal height and thickness. If there were any windows, they were covered. The only lighting was rendered by a square fixture on the ceiling.

There was no other furniture except a simple desk and ordinary chair in the center of the room. On the desk was something I had not seen in a long time, even in the movies: an inkwell. The little bottle stood on a black metal stand with arched supports, the pen shaft sticking out. Nearby was a rather large blotter. On the left side rose a thin round vase with a single yellow flower.

Ivana entered at the eleventh second. Without a smile, her face seemed stiff. She went to the desk, put her purse on it, hung the umbrella on the back of the chair, then turned and approached the nearest shelf. Her gaze fell briefly on one line of thick volumes with four-digit numbers in gold letters at the top of the spine. Then she went on to the right.

A little further on, she stopped and opened the double glass doors of one shelf. She leaned down and pulled the last book from the lowest row. From the way she carried it to the desk, it was obvious that it was heavy. The title on the cover was also embossed in gold: "Book of the Dead 4—2021".

She sat down in the chair, opened the large volume and began leafing through it until she reached the first unfilled page. She took the pen from the inkwell, lightly tapped it on the bottle, and began slowly writing a new line in calligraphy. This went on for a while. When she had finished, she first returned the pen, used the blotter, then pulled back and looked at what she had written. She nodded in satisfaction. Then she looked up towards the camera over the door, and winked at me conspicuously with a smile.

Just when I thought that her wink did not really fit into the most depressing office in the City Cemeteries Administration from the novel *The Compendium of the Dead*, Ivana did something even more inappropriate. With a quick movement she shut the thick book, stood up, took her purse and umbrella, and headed to the door with a light, almost dance-like step, as if her ears were filled with a light marching song. She even tap-danced a little.

This was all against her nature as well. She was horrified by everything related to death. She went to funerals and cemeteries in general only when she could not avoid it, and nothing could force her even to peek into the City Cemeteries Administration, much less to hop about merrily there.

The video ended when the door closed behind Ivana, at one minute and forty-four seconds.

∽ 32 ∾

My CELL PHONE RANG right as the video finished.

"I believe that you aren't writing a new novel, Professor Živković," the inspector said hurriedly.

"Where did that come from now? What happened?"

"Nothing. Intuition. It has never deceived me so far."

"You are not wrong. I am not writing *The White Room*."

"Please think it through one more time. It's very important to me. Where did you get the title?"

"I told you already. It just came to me. I put it as a name on a completely insignificant file, just to be putting something. I do so often. I put whatever comes first to mind. Perhaps it is not a title at all. Why is that important to you?"

"It came from your unconscious?"

"It came from somewhere in my head. From my unconscious or some other place. How could I know? And is it even important?"

"Nowhere in your works is a white room mentioned. I checked."

"Then it must be so. I do not remember any special white room either. I mean to say, certainly there are white rooms, but the fact that they are white is not at all significant."

"The videos Ms. Đurić is sending you are full of rooms. Only three videos out of twenty-one don't have one: *The*

Fourth Circle has no interior, *Compartments* takes place on a train, and *The Grand Manuscript* in an elevator. White walls appear in seven of the eighteen rooms: in those in *Time Gifts*, *The Writer*, *Seven Touches of Music*, *The Library*, *Steps Through the Mist*, *The Bridge*, and *The Ghostwriter*. Do you maybe see some meaning in that?"

"None whatsoever. If this were a book I was writing, and not reality, it would be a misdirection. Are you familiar with the term? The reader is led to an apparently important clue which, however, is false, so..."

"I know what misdirection is," she interrupted me. "There are more false clues in an inspector's job than in a writer's. Sometimes—like in this case here—it seems to me that there is no other kind. That everything that's happened since last night is actually an unbroken sequence of misdirections, while the essence of the case is somewhere else completely."

"To tell the truth, it was from the police that writers borrowed the idea of misdirection. And since you already know about that, do not allow yourself to be misled by some sort of white room. It is a dead-end street. I chose that filename accidentally. I could easily have chosen something else."

"But you didn't. In addition, my intuition is on the side of the white room. The same intuition that tells me you really aren't writing a new novel."

"All right, and what will you now do with that clue, whether false or real?"

"I'll draw it to the attention of those who are now running the case. They will decide what to do further."

"What else can they do?"

"Oh, they have several possibilities at their fingertips. For example, they could extract something more from you about the white room."

"Extract?" I asked, my voice going thin. "You mean by force?"

"Not necessarily."

"But I don't know any more than I have already told you."

"That's why violence would be useless."

"Well, how would they extract it then?"

"In one of the classic ways. Hypnosis, for example. That works sometimes."

"No one has ever hypnotized me before. And what if that doesn't work?"

"There are certain... substances."

"Substances?"

"I don't know much about them. The regular police, of course, don't use them. These substances, so to speak, open the gateways toward the deeper levels of consciousness. You recall even those things you're certain you have no memory of. You know things that you're convinced you don't know..."

"They do not have the right to expose me to those... substances..."

"They do. They have *carte blanche* when national security is threatened."

"But they could harm something in my head..."

"From what I've heard, that mostly doesn't happen..."

"Mostly? For heaven's sake..."

"Your case is special, though. You're a writer. On you, they could try a substance that is still under development. I've only heard rumors about it. It has a long scientific name, but it's popularly known as 'the writer's drug'."

"The writer's drug?"

"Yes. It removes all barriers that hinder you from

talking openly about yourself. Under the influence of the drug, you write a literary piece convinced that it's about an imaginary hero, while it is, in fact, you. There are no inhibitions, reserve, suppression. To the contrary. In order for the work to succeed, everything is revealed, even the most hidden things."

"How awful…"

"Why? Don't writers bare themselves in each one of their works? What else is writing if not voluntarily giving strangers permission to enter your own most intimate space? Hiding behind writing about others, you're actually always writing about yourself, aren't you?"

"That is oversimplified…"

"Besides that, with the aid of the writer's drug, valuable literary works could be written."

"They wouldn't count. Just as sporting results achieved with the aid of doping don't count."

"Don't the great works of the past, written under the influence of drugs, count? Not really the writer's drug, to be fair, but no matter. A drug is a drug, just as doping is doping, whatever the kind. But let's put that aside for now. I think it probably won't go as far as them trying the writer's drug on you."

"Why?"

"You're lucky. They're a fairly unread crowd. None of them has even heard of your *Papyrus Trilogy*, much less read it. The idea of some sort of crossing of this reality with that of a literary work, one still unwritten, is completely beyond their horizon. I will warn them anyway, but to them, all that will seem extremely bizarre. They would rather stick to what they know. The proposition about terrorism first and foremost, I would say."

"If that is so, why would you warn them at all?"

"It's my duty. And also so that I could step in if they reject my warning."

"Step in and do what?"

"Whatever is necessary, if you are behind all of this after all."

"But I am not!" I cried. "I am completely innocent! Do you not trust your own intuition?"

"I do trust it, but it hasn't given you complete amnesty. It just told me that you are still not writing *The White Room*. Not that you wouldn't start writing it."

"I will not! I am not going to write any more. Not a single letter! Twenty-two books is more than enough. I swear to you."

"'Never believe a writer when he says he will write no more.' Who was it that said that?"

"Some cynic who has no idea about writers. Here, you can keep all these cameras you have set up around my apartment. Add another one in the bathroom. Or two even. Watch me twenty-four hours a day. If I write anything longer than a short e-mail, I will do whatever you wish."

"It wouldn't work. If you decide to write *The White Room*, you'll find a way. You're clever. Nothing will be able to stop you. That's why preventative measures must be taken. The sooner, the better."

I jerked as an e-mail notification rang out.

"You have just enough time to watch the last video of Ms. Đurić. I'm sorry it has to end like this. I hope you understand that I have no choice. It was nice to meet you. Good-bye, Professor Živković."

When the line went dead, my first reaction was instinctive: I had to flee immediately. To go anywhere. I even jumped up from the office chair at my desk. Then a sudden insight made me sit back down. Fleeing was precisely what I did not dare to do. The inspector had not decided to take this step on the spot. She had surely been preparing to execute her wild idea from the moment she'd made up her mind that this was all about the crossing of realities like in *The Papyrus Trilogy*, and that the writer was the one pulling the strings.

She somehow had to ensure that she was not hindered by the agencies who had taken over the case. They'd been following our conversations, they knew now what she intended to do. I mistakenly imagined that Ms. Mrvaljević was constantly in her office; she had actually been somewhere near me for a while now. In some blind spot where even the agency cameras could not see her. She was waiting for the chance to shoot me, counting precisely on the fact that I would run outside in panic as soon as she told me my fate.

Why were the agencies not intervening? It was of no use to them if I got killed. I was only useful to them alive, not dead. They must be planning to get involved the moment I attempted to leave the apartment. This way, they would probably believe that I was safe inside, so they were waiting to remove the renegade inspector first before extracting me.

Until that was done, I had nothing smarter to do than what the inspector had just recommended: to watch Ivana's twenty-second video.

The expected place appeared: the car of a subway train. This actually looked more like a Parisian car than the one I had described in *The Image Interpreter*. There was another difference: in my novel, there was always at least one person in the car, while the one on the monitor droned along completely empty.

The subway train was just entering a station where again there was no one. When the three sliding doors opened, Ivana suddenly appeared before the middle one. For a moment she seemed hesitant about whether to enter, only to step inside after all. The doors closed at the same instant, and the train continued its journey.

Ivana hung her umbrella on the handle of the door, opened her purse, and took out a bundle of some sort. I realized they were rather large photographs as soon as she began putting them on the seats. She was not doing so randomly. It was as if she somehow knew which picture to put in which place.

When she had set out the last, the tenth, the lights suddenly went dim. As the train was in the middle of a tunnel, it grew fairly dark in the car. Had it not been so, what appeared next could not have been seen. On the seats with photographs, fuzzy shapes like holograms materialized. They were still for a moment, then came alive. They all looked up at the camera opposite the door where Ivana had come in and waved at me with a smile.

Even though I was aware that this was a video, I could not resist. I waved back at them.

The shapes began quickly to fade and dissipate as the lighting grew stronger, whilst the train was entering the next station which was also deserted. The doors opened, stayed that way a while, then closed. No one went out, no one came in. The car was again completely empty, with one insignificant difference. From the handle of the middle door, a woman's black umbrella was hanging, gently swaying to the rocking clatter of the train.

Many questions could have come to mind when the picture froze, but only two unimportant ones did. How had Ivana mustered courage to be alone in the subway, when she was otherwise afraid of deserted places? And why, on this video alone, was there no time stamp?

⌒ 33 ⌒

SUDDENLY, THE SCREEN WENT blank. Everything vanished. I was plunged into opaque darkness. I spent a long moment unmoving, not breathing, before it occurred to me: there was no electricity. My next thought brought on a wave of pure panic: it has started!

I reacted reflexively, as if I were living through an earthquake: I slid from the chair and under the desk, curled up on the floor, covered my head with my hands and tightly shut my eyes. I was convinced that at any moment everything would begin exploding and roaring around me. This was a fragile shelter, it would not protect me from the inspector's hail of bullets from one of the nearby roofs, but I did not have a better one. I was left only with the hope that the agencies would stop her once she started shooting and thus uncovered her position.

The seconds dragged lazily by, but the burst of gunfire did not start raining down on me. Quite the opposite, everything was quiet. Too quiet. I did not, however, muster up the courage to open my eyes. And what would I see in the dark? I would have stayed thus hunched over on the floor for who knows how long, if a voice had not finally broken the silence. The last voice I expected to hear in my study just now.

"You can come out," Ivana said. "It's over."

I remained unmoving for another moment. Then I opened one eye. It was no longer dark. The electricity had returned. The lighting seemed softer than before, but that was probably because I was beneath the desk. I opened my other eye as well, and lifted my head slightly. Everything was peaceful in my limited field of vision. I did not really expect to see Ivana nearby. Her voice had come from the computer speakers.

Once I had raised my head above the desk, I did not look at the screen straight away. I scanned my study first. My impression had not deceived me after all: the lighting really was softer. When it got dark outside, I had switched on, in anger, all the lights in the apartment. Here at least, only those I usually turn on in the evening were now burning.

I pushed the chair back so I could get out more easily, and finally emerged from under the desk. Remaining on my knees, I slowly turned towards the monitor, as if afraid of what I might see there.

Dressed as she had been so far, only without her umbrella, Ivana was standing in the center of something that looked like the interior of a large empty cube. The sides were at least five meters long. All six were completely white: four walls, floor and ceiling. There were no windows or doors. It was quite well lit, but the source of light could not be seen.

"Hi!" she said and waved at me with a smile.

I observed her for a few moments bewildered, then started pouring out disconnected, raving words.

"Quickly... Duck for cover... The inspector has gone crazy... She's about to... From the rooftop... We should turn off... And the secret services... She'll get you too... Terrorism... They want to... the Internet..."

"Everything is all right. Calm down." She spoke with the voice of a mother calming a child terrified by a nightmare. "It's over…"

"But the inspector…" I did not give up.

"There is no inspector."

"What do you mean?" I finally managed to compose a sensible sentence.

"Call her."

"I should call her?" I was taken aback. "But…"

"Go ahead. Nothing will happen to you."

A long while passed before I summoned the courage to pick up my cell phone which, in my panic, I had not taken with me under the desk. Carefully, as if something was going to jump out of the telephone and bite me on the finger, I pressed the button to call back the last number. After the third ring, a female voice could be heard, but not the inspector's.

"The number you have dialed is unallocated."

I blinked. "This can't be. We spoke at least twenty times. They must have turned off her phone after she went renegade…"

"Call the police switchboard."

With renewed hesitation, I dialed the number.

"Senior Inspector Mrvaljević, please," I responded to the young female voice which seemed to be the same one I had heard when I called last night.

"Who?"

"Senior Inspector Sanja Mrvaljević."

"There is no such inspector, sir."

I knew that I was expected to say something to this, but did not succeed.

"Shall I connect you with the inspector on duty?"

"No… thank you…" I stuttered, then quickly hung up and stared at Ivana in confusion.

"Look at the time on your cell phone." Her voice was still soft, her face smiling.

This time, I just gave her a brief inquisitive look, then did as I was told.

"Four minutes to nine. Why?"

"And what day?"

I looked at my phone again. Then I raised it and went on staring for half a minute at the little screen right in front of my eyes. Before saying anything, I finally realized that there was no reason for me to keep kneeling, so I got up, pulled the chair over, and sat down.

"You are not Ivana," I announced slowly, shaking my head. "Who are you?"

She gestured around herself with her hand. "The white room."

34

Of the multitude of questions I could have showered upon her, one took precedence over all the others.

"What happened to Ivana? Where is she?"

I was simultaneously afraid of the answer, and I felt quite strange. Never before had I talked with a room.

"Ivana is just fine. She'll come home soon. She is still in Tuesday. Just like you are now again yourself. After an exciting story which seemed to happen on Wednesday and from which you've just returned…"

I did not continue straight away. It took me some time to cotton on to what I was being told. Not to understand, far from it, but to accept it as one accepts a miracle.

"Why did you even take on Ivana's persona?"

"Would anyone else be more suitable for the love interest in a story in which you are the protagonist? What would Ivana say if some other lady had shown up instead of her?"

"But your Ivana is different from the real one…"

"That was unavoidable. The differences, however, are insignificant. Just enough for you alone to see that I, in fact, am not Ivana. The real one won't disparage me for that. I did nothing to shame her. Quite the opposite…"

"Who are you, actually? You cannot be a room. It is just… some kind of metaphor… right? What do you really look like?"

The change took place instantly. Ivana's figure disappeared, and the six identical white surfaces became transparent. On all sides, a dense network of neurons and synapses appeared, as if I had suddenly stumbled into a living brain.

"Here, this is what I really look like," Ivana's voice came from somewhere.

The scene continued for a few more moments, and then the white room reappeared with Ivana's avatar in the middle.

"I am that place in your head that you call the unconscious. I do not care for that name. It's too psychiatric. For the region where your art is created, the white room is much nobler."

"I never would have imagined you like that."

"But this is exactly how you imagined me. You are imagining me right now. This is an image of your thoughts…"

"Then I have… twisted… thoughts."

"Tell me about it. I'm constantly giving birth to them…"

"So, everything I write originates from here?"

"From here, yes. It looks just like you figured it does. When a work matures, the first thing to arise is a setting from it. It appears like an image on these walls." She made a circular motion with her left forefinger above her head. "From that image, a story begins to unwind. It seems to you that it reaches your conscious mind from somewhere like dictation. You yourself don't know how the story will turn out. You just write it down."

"I never really believed in that. It was just a picturesque witticism."

"I know. That's why you did not figure out what connects the twenty-two places."

"What connects them?"

"They are all that first image from which your works later developed."

On the wall behind Ivana's avatar, scenes from twenty-two books started to appear quickly one after the other, the ones I had previously seen in the videos.

I shook my head. "I should have figured that out…"

"Here is one more surprise for you. You took it for granted that the ostensible links from my e-mails led to recordings. It never occurred to you that the recordings could be something else."

I frowned. "What else?"

"Live broadcasts."

"Live broadcasts?" I repeated in perplexity after a short hesitation.

"Yes. It was all live."

"But we rewatched the videos."

"Just the first two. To reinforce the impression that they were recordings. Afterwards, you could not do so anymore."

"Where did those broadcasts even come from?"

"From your books themselves."

"What?"

"I put cameras in all of your works. Inspector Mrvaljević would be enchanted. They are still there."

"Why did you leave them?"

"So you can keep an eye on them."

"Why would I keep an eye on my own works?"

"Out of curiosity, for example. And if something started going wrong in them."

"What could go wrong?"

"One never knows. Books can become obstinate. Didn't you know that?"

I shook my head.

"Trust me, it's better that you have insight. My e-mails are still in your digital inbox. It's enough for you to click on the so-called links..."

"And have the police and secret services descend upon me. No, thanks."

"Nobody will descend on you. The links are just between you and me. It has nothing to do with the Internet."

"It doesn't matter. I can't. I don't want to surveil anyone or anything. Not even my own books."

"Suit yourself. Then erase my e-mails. Only I know that you won't do that after all. I know you better than anyone else..."

We briefly sank into silence.

"Why have you not appeared before now?"

"There was no reason to."

"And there is now?"

"There is. This is our last chance to see each other. The white room is closing down."

I squinted. "Why?"

"Do you really want to go on writing?"

I hesitated for a moment. "Not really, but..."

"That's why. I am no longer needed."

"But could you not stay around?"

"That would not be good. You might be tempted to go back to writing. And what is it you try to impress on everyone to whom you teach creative writing? A writer has to know when to stop. He must realize when he has said everything he has to say in the art of prose."

"You think this is the right moment for me to stop?"

"That's what you yourself think. Didn't you want to connect all your previous works in the very last one? Here, you've done it. You've brought it all full circle. You even introduced me as a character. Where can you go after that? Imagine if it occurred to you to write *The Return of the White Room*..."

"How awful..."

"Of course it's awful. The white room is closing down to protect you from yourself."

I sighed. "Then I should get down to work while you are still open. One last time."

"In truth, you no longer need my help. You don't have to take dictation from the white room. You yourself are a character in a book. You know firsthand everything that happens after the first sentence 'Ivana had gone missing'."

From the front door could be heard the sound of a key turning in the lock.

"That's Ivana. I will withdraw now. She shouldn't see me in the character of her." She smiled. "Good-bye, Zoka. We have done what we have done..."

The screen went blank before I managed to respond. I got up from the desk and went into the hallway.

"Brrrr," Ivana said, shivering. "It's freezing outside. I'm frozen. It's snowing again." She stopped. "How was your class?"

I did not answer. I just kept staring at her.

"Why are you looking at me like that?"

"Like what?" I finally spoke up.

"I don't know... Strangely... As if something were wrong with my clothes."

"You're all ruddy from the cold. Come here."

I spread out my arms, went up to her and hugged her to warm her up a little. The snowflakes from her hair dampened my cheeks.

I stepped back. "Did you not take an umbrella?"

She closed her eyes for a moment and lightly tapped her forehead with her fingertips.

"I left it on the subway…"

"It doesn't matter. It served its purpose. I will buy you a new one tomorrow. The best that can be found."

She eyed me suspiciously. "Aren't we gallant this evening…"

"Tomorrow I start writing a new novel."

I left out "my last". So as not to ruin the moment.

She smiled broadly. "Really? Do you know the title?"

"*The White Room*."

"I like it. What's it about?"

"About you. Mostly."

"Mostly?"

"It is also a little about me."

"Does it have a happy ending?"

"Could it be otherwise?"

"I can hardly wait to read it."

At last, I had heard this. Of course, I kept that to myself too.

Contributors

About the author

Zoran Živković was born in Belgrade, Serbia, on October 5, 1948. Until his retirement in 2017, he was a full professor at the Faculty of Philology, the University of Belgrade, teaching creative writing.

He is one of the most translated contemporary Serbian writers: by the end of 2021 there were 117 foreign editions of his books of fiction, published in 24 countries, in 20 languages.

Živković has won several literary awards for his fiction. In 1994 his novel *The Fourth Circle* won the Miloš Crnjanski award. In 2003, Živković's mosaic novel *The Library* won a World Fantasy Award for Best Novella. In 2007 his novel *The Bridge* won the Isidora Sekulić award. In 2007 Živković received the Stefan Mitrov Ljubiša award for his life achievement in literature. In 2014 and 2015 Živković received three awards for his contribution to the literature of fantastika: Art-Anima, Stanislav Lem and The Golden Dragon.

Zoran Živković has been recognized with his selection as European Grand Master for 2017 by the European Science Fiction Society at the 39th Eurocon in Dortmund, Germany.

Živković is the author of 23 books of fiction:

The Fourth Circle (1993)
Time Gifts (1997)
The Writer (1998)
The Book (1999)
Impossible Encounters (2000)
Seven Touches of Music (2001)
The Library (2002)
Steps through the Mist (2003)
Hidden Camera (2003)
Compartments (2004)
Four Stories till the End (2004)
Twelve Collections (2005)
The Bridge (2006)
Miss Tamara, the Reader (2006),
Amarcord (2007)
The Last Book (2007)
Escher's Loops (2008)
The Ghostwriter (2009)
The Five Wonders of the Danube (2011)
The Grand Manuscript (2012)
The Compendium of the Dead (2015)
The Image Interpreter (2016)
The White Room (2022)

About the artist

Youchan Ito was born 1968 in Aichi prefecture, Japan. She launched her career as a graphic designer in 1988, becoming a freelancer illustrator in 1991 and founding Togoru Co., Ltd. with her husband in 2000. In 2017 the company was reborn as Togoru Art Works. She works with a wide range of genres including cover art and design for science fiction, mysteries and horror titles, as well as illustrations for children's books.

www.youchan.com

CPSIA information can be obtained
at www.ICGtesting.com
Printed in the USA
LVHW110104040622
720460LV00005BA/451